Harriet Eleanor Hamilton King

Aspromonte

And other Poems

Harriet Eleanor Hamilton King

Aspromonte
And other Poems

ISBN/EAN: 9783337158538

Printed in Europe, USA, Canada, Australia, Japan

Cover: Foto ©Andreas Hilbeck / pixelio.de

More available books at **www.hansebooks.com**

ASPROMONTE

AND OTHER POEMS.

London:

MACMILLAN AND CO.

1869.

PREFACE.

THESE POEMS were written several years ago, between the ages of eighteen and twenty-two. This is mentioned, not as an irrelevant extenuation of their faults, but as some explanation of their peculiarities. Their publication has been deferred, in the hope that following years might produce better work: but circumstances having led to a different development, they are now put forward with the hope that they may find a few friends before they are quite out of date.

June 16, 1869.

CONTENTS.

POEMS FOR ITALY.

DRAMATIC LYRICS.

Contents.

MISCELLANEOUS.

POEMS FOR ITALY.

B

GARIBALDI—but his charm is overthrown,
    Garibaldi—but his flag is in the dust,
Garibaldi—but a prisoner to his own,
    Garibaldi—but foredoom'd by sentence just.
Garibaldi—but a criminal and fool,
Garibaldi—but the world's faith has grown cool;
Garibaldi—but a name for scoffs and scorns,
    For the pity and the moral of the wise,
But the laurel leaves have sharpen'd into thorns,
    But the Lion low with his lost fortune lies;
Garibaldi—but in helpless wounded pain,
Garibaldi—but the fallen, never to rise again.

Garibaldi, but you are yourself for ever!
    But you never were so noble and so dear;
Garibaldi, but Christ neither now nor ever
    Has loos'd His hand from holding yours to cheer:
But the Comforter is with you all the while,
Making still your silence radiant with your smile;

Garibaldi, but you are our own, our Master,
  But the little ones and foolish cleave to you,
But around our fallen Hero we close faster,
  But now i' this dark hour truer are the true.
Garibaldi, but we love you, we adore you,
Garibaldi, but our hearts are breaking for you ;
But the Right endureth, though the Wrong prevaileth,
Garibaldi—God is with you still when this world faileth.

—

High on Aspromonte flashed the red shirts early,
  Up in the midst of them the glory of his face.
Low on Aspromonte, ere the day was over,
  He was down and bleeding, bound in helpless case.
Hands of brothers pour'd that crimson—nevermore
Tears can wash it from the holy Tricolor.
  Alas ! Alas ! could they hit him where he stood,
    Himself thrown between the ranks, with passionate
      cries
  Calling on them but to spare each other's blood,
    And so, falling, gave himself a sacrifice.
O, the pity and the passion of that morrow,
  When, all lost, all ended, he th' invincible
Lay there stricken in his ruin and his sorrow,
  Prisoner in the hands of those he loved too well.

Over rugged mountain-paths without complaint
Carried through long hours of torture, white and faint,
   By the faithful, silent in his silence all,
   Marching slow and soft as at a funeral.
Overhead all day the scorching August quiver'd,
   While the laurel leaves look'd sadness, shading him,
As they bore him from the land he had deliver'd,
   Helpless, shatter'd, hot with anguish heart and limb ;
No salute, or sign, or murmur as he passed ;
But once, looking up, he waved his hand at last :
Farewell !—kneeling on the shore the people shiver'd,
   Stretching out their hands long after the white sails
     had grown dim.

How have they received him back to his own country ?
   He, the man who threw himself into the front for those
Who, standing aloof, let him bear the peril only,
   And now have forsaken him when the rough wind
     blows.
Has the King himself come forth to welcome him,
   Remembering the kingdom that he gave him ?
Have they made a palace ready for him ?
   Could they not comfort if they could not save him ?
   Did they not crown him first ere they forgave him !—
Courts of law to judge the rebel and to try him,
   Prison portion for the criminal found due,

Haste officious to disown him and deny him,
  This is royal recompense for service over true.

There on Varignano frowns the fortress where
  Italy keeps her captive, weeping over him ;
Passive, his part over, in their ward and care,
  If perchance they may even yet recover him.
Through the damp and gloomy prison walls we go
  To the chamber where they have laid him to endure,
  Faded, and bare to the North, forlorn and poor ;
Open doors, and many footsteps passing to and fro,
  Anxious looks, and undertones, and busy hands ;
And in the midst of them a narrow bed and low,
And a pale face leaning upwards—the face that we all
    know,—
  A pallid face with its own smile, that lightens all the
    lands.
Looking into his eyes, the shadow and storm are past;
Not a word to utter, our wild tears come too fast;
It is yourself, Garibaldi—we have kiss'd your hand at last.

Lying pallid with his face to the heavens,
  Swooning silently under the surgeon's knife,
Pierc'd to the soul where he looked for comfort,
  Dimly eclipse boding over his life ;
Wasted away in the sleepless fever—

But the lip still set in its calm of old,
Child-like caressing, serene as ever,
Patient as heretofore pitiful-soul'd :—
And we know that deep into heaven those absent eyes
behold.

Do we understand you, Garibaldi?
    Truly, I think not so.
We rejoice in you, we would die for you,
    Where you go, we would go ;
Near you we feel nearer heaven :
    Is not that enough to know?
Can the lesser contain the greater?
    For ever the law says, ' No.'
Even if over his forehead
    It were not sculptured plain,
How in perfect power harmonious
    The heart is match'd with the brain ;
Must we break in pieces the grandeur
    That we cannot receive?
God is not us'd, half finished
    His noblest works to leave.
And yet there are some among us
    Who, claiming respect and rule,
Can smile and say : ' What a pity
    A hero should be a fool.'

O, foolish Garibaldi !
   That might have been cross'd and starr'd
With diamonds, and set among princes,
   And had gold for his reward ;
And chooses rather in prison
   To be lying stiff and scarr'd,
His fortunes all risked headlong,
   Ruthlessly crush'd and marr'd,
With his name from its marvellous glory
   Fall'n in the world's regard,
And his own whom he saved, upon him
   Sitting in judgment hard.

Rose-coloured Republic of Christ !
   So long in coming to pass ;
So long that our hearts are weary,
   And our faith grows cold, alas !
But to this the nations are yearning
   In their fever and complaint ;
And for this the silent workers
   In their patience do not faint.
And for thirty years one Prophet,
   Rejected, despised, abhorr'd,
Has been crying in the wilderness :
   ' Make straight the way of the Lord ! '
And yet we go on blindly

Caring not to understand,
Nor to lift our eyes to the letters
  Trac'd out by the shining hand.
But surely we need that vision
  To interpret what is dark ;
As he sees it, his face set forward,
  Fearlessly on to the mark.

For we need discipline, guidance,
  Restraints and rigours of rule ;
And only a few of the foremost
  Are coming out of school.
But another kingdom is coming,
  Whose dawn is in the sky,
And they who watch on the mountains
  Have a vision that it is nigh ;
Light, light through the mists is breaking,
  So that all may walk thereby !
Already in far-off echoes
  The new glory thrilling o'er us ;
' The Lord shall reign for ever and ever ! '
  Swelling on in marvellous chorus ;
The blue of the heavens upbuilding
  A mighty temple before us.
And over the arch is written
  In letters orient-gilt,

The perfect law of liberty:
'Love, and do what thou wilt.'

And he is of that kingdom:
The glory around his head
Is only the ray auroral
By which his footsteps are led.
Not that he himself is greater
Than other men might be;
All by toilsome ways will later
Arrive where now stands he;
But that, loving, therefore living
The life divinely true,
Without law or line, unerring,
Single-hearted he goes through:
Standing before our Father
With the heart of a little child,
Perfect duty and perfect freedom
In that clear faith reconcil'd;
And that, walking amid shadows
That wait for a higher birth,
He acts in its presence already
As though it were come on earth,
Type and token of the future,
To the famishing of dearth.

And therefore the world's heart throbs to him,
  In conscious travail and pain,
Stretching out her hands and tossing,
  Till her Lord shall come again.
And therefore the poor and simple,
  In their weakness and distress,
With passionate blind devotion,
  Around him kneel and press,
Feeling themselves made sacred
  In his reverent tenderness.
The heart of the people, breaking,
  Knows its own woe and need;
'The brother of Jesus Christ,' they say,
  Poor, pining souls indeed!

You have given him your love, Italy!
  It was all he would take from you:
Well may you weep and wail his hurt,
  Who trusted that you were true!
Had you, now bitterly rueing,
  Been worthy of him, alas!
This deed, which has no undoing,
  Would never have come to pass.
When he came forward, giving
  The signal forth, Be men!

Did he look for such an answer
  To be given him back again?
What was that small love-token
  You sent him the other day,
So that, bone and sinew broken,
  Struck down to earth he lay?
Could you find nothing more tender
  Than a bullet to kiss his feet?
Strange homage for you to render!
  When fronting once more you meet,
How will you look at your lover
  Halt of step and pale of cheek?
Surely your face you must cover
  Though never reproach he speak.

There is One in Heaven, Garibaldi,
  Whose face we have not seen:
But thinner to you than to us lies
  The veil that hangs between.
He has made you for His own work;
  He has kept you spotless through;
And you know better than we can,
  What He has called you to do:
Some day you will go forth again,
  And He will go with you.

Aspromonte.

If we would but look up, to us
    The heavens would open too !

Now, courage !   Has his cause with him
    Gone down in this overthrow ?
Are works and prayers thrown backwards;
    And all in vain ?   Oh no !
Those eyes that see the farthest
    Declare that it is not so.
How often we know already,
    When the arm of the conqueror fails,
When the wise have sunk despairing,
    The martyr at last prevails.
So our hopes are with you, whether
    Your fortunes rise or fall;
For you are Garibaldi,
    And God is over all !

THE

EXECUTION OF FELICE ORSINI,

March 13th, 1858.

' Fuor se' dell' erte vie, fuor se' dell' arte.'—DANTE.

PART I.

THE STREETS OF PARIS.

A DAY to be much remembered,
    Sad and sublime;
Written in letters of red
    In the book of Time.
Not a coronation morning,
    With its light of purple and gold,
And floods of mighty music
    In hallelujahs rolled :
Not a young bride led home
    From royal halls afar,
All pallid and pearl-glittering,
    A sweet and tremulous Star:

Not a conqueror's State entry,
　　With his armies marching back
Under triumphal arches,
　　A glittering scarlet track,
When the wide streets glare in sunshine,
　　And the bells ring out all day,
And the people shout together,
　　Knowing not what they say :—
Only a winter's morning,
　　Crowds standing silent by,
A prison and a scaffold,
　　And a man brought out to die.

In the cold, damp darkness,
　　Between the night and day,
With nerv'd and solemn heart,
　　Forth we take our way
To follow to thy martyrdom—
　　Last homage we can pay;
To watch with our own eyes
　　The setting of this star;
To bear thee faithful company
　　Down this dark road, as far
As where the soul and God
　　Alone together are.

Paris is all astir;
Another day for her
  Of tragedy.
Sunrise is not for long,
Yet onward pours along
The ever-thickening throng
  Continually.
Fresh streams from every street
A ceaseless press of feet,
In quick and countless beat;
  All one way they fare.
The darkness seems alive—
  A breathing, moving thing.
With a strange awe we strive:
  This hollow murmuring
    In the damp, leaden air,
This vague and heaving sea
  Of shadows undefin'd,
Hurrying confusedly,
  Seems every sense to bind
In nightmare weight of gloom;
For silently they come:
A horror-quiet broods
Over the multitudes;—
No wild cries—no word

Above their breath is heard:
The air is only stirred
    By a vague whispering hum.

Sudden and startling comes
A long, loud roll of drums;
    And the echo clear
Of bugle notes afar
Winds down the Boulevards:
    Be ready—the hour is near!
Through the darkness and the damp,
On comes the clatter and tramp
    Of the squadrons down the street:
A shock—a rushing past;
Furiously and fast
    The heavy, hurrying feet
Over the stones are sped.
' To guard the scaffold,' said
    A voice beside us, low.
Did ye not mark it when
    They pass'd the lamp below—
  How cold and blue the steel
  Flash'd out ?—Did ye not feel
A sudden shrinking then?
    And the ring of spurs and reins
    Came like the clank of chains.

Heaven help us all this day!
Would we were far away.
Already, in foreshadowing,
  Our spirits sink and cower;
Yet *he* has given up all things
  To suffer death this hour.

The light becomes more clear;
The daybreak draweth near,
Yet brings no warmth to cheer,
  Nor sunrise glow.
No sun will shine to-day;
The dark fogs drift away;
The skies are leaden grey,
  Sullen and low;
White and ghostly sheets
Of mist hang o'er the streets,
  Wet with trodden snow.
Dismaller and drearer
Ever as we draw nearer
  Seems the way to grow.
To the great burial garden
  Onward now it turns;
Past long lines of tombstones,
  And cold funeral urns;

Where the living have made
Of the dead a trade.
Bare, bleach'd crosses stand
Stiff on either hand,
Showing dismal white
In the chill half-light.
    All things black and dolorous :—
      Coffins with sable pall;
    Dark plumes and hearse-trappings,
      Heavy on every wall;
    A horror of the charnel-house
      Overshadowing all ;—
    Only the pallid Immortelles
      Some brighter thoughts recall;
    Fresh and fair, yet never a wreath
      But tears thereon shall fall.
    And if the way were clear,
      As three hours hence 'twill be,
    The cypress at the gates
      Before us we might see,
    Guarding that sad harvest field,
      Sown darkly in decay,
    Where twenty generations
      Are mouldering to clay.
    But we will leave them, lying
      In their desolate array—

Not of the Dead, but the Dying,
    Our hearts are full to-day.

Now we are close at hand :
    Before us outlined dimly
    La Roquette rises grimly,
    Black as death and sorrow—
    Holy ground to-morrow.
Countless thousands stand
    Already crowded there,
    Filling the open square,
    And stretching every side
    Far up the streetways wide,
        Till, lost in gloom and haze,
    The vague, dim, human tide
        With shadowy motion sways ;
    Who motionless and still,
        While even he has slept,
        Through the night-frosts have kept
    Their vigils faint and chill.
        They gather'd yester-eve,
    When the snow began to fall ;
The long, dark hours toll'd heavily,
    Standing they counted all,
And the day dawns on pale faces
    Waiting to see him fall.

Nor these perhaps alone
This night has wakeful known.
　　The lamps burn on the altars
　　　　In the churches all night long;
Surely some pious souls
　　　　Have stay'd since evensong
To pray for the passing soul—
　　　　Christ, shrive him from his wrong!—
O! all good souls and true,
Spare him a prayer or two,—
　　'Tis but little while ye may;
Grudge not of tears a few,
He gives his blood for you,
　　He is dying to-day.
The light that flash'd all Europe through
　　Is vanishing away—
The arm that like the lightning flew
Wherever there was work to do, ,
Braving all pain and peril anew.—
O God! Thou know'st his heart was true
　　　　Even in this offence!
　　Then watch for one hour longer,
　　　　One hour yet more intense,
　　In this dark mid-lent season,
　　　　For him who goeth hence;—

The haughty hero-spirit,
　　Parting in penitence.

While in the Tuileries,
Sleepless and ill at ease,
Silent as Fate's decrees,
　　As morn came on;
Waiting till all was o'er,
Through hall and corridor
Restless the Emperor
　　Pac'd up and down;
Thinking we know not what;
If sorrow, utter'd not.—
Emperor! have you forgot,
Thinking of him, one day
Long ago, years away,
　　Nearer the morning skies,
When under one command
He and you took your stand
Comrades, and, hand in hand,
　　Look'd in each other's eyes;—
At your own peril, both
Utter'd the same high oath,
Self-doom'd for broken troth,
　　Then parted from each other?
Since then, through chance and change,
Each by rough ways and strange,

Ye to the goal have past
Separate ; and now, at last,
Once more your fates are cast
   In the world's eye together.
Each doom'd, by fortune's stress,
By each, yet not the less
Too great for bitterness ;
Still that bond feels unrent,
Through all between that went,
By that old sacrament,
   He is your brother.
Those days when truth seem'd true,
One vow was on you two ;
He has kept his—and *you?*
   Now, past recall
He goes ; when next you meet
At the same Judge's feet,
Your work will be complete ;—
   Hear you no call?

There, on the farther side,
   Before the prison gates,
The scaffold yet undy'd,
   The sacrifice awaits ;
All the eyes around
Thereon are strain'd and bound,

Where the hideous frame
  Rises gaunt and tall,
Its cords wound up for working,
  Dull red painted all ;
The hard block ready laid,
The overhanging blade,
  Horrible they loom
  Through the thinning gloom.
    Who now feels heart among us
  To tempt this visible doom ?
    A wide-swept space around
    Of clear'd and open ground,
    By guards on three sides bound ;
Deep files on either hand,
Flank'd by the horsemen stand,
      An iron wall ;
Rein'd steeds in close lines drawn,
Naked swords upright borne,
Helmets on fierce brows worn,
      Motionless all.
  Driven back by armed stress,
  Surging, the people press ;
From every house in Paris
    Every man has come—
Some as to a spectacle,
    As to an altar some ;

Careless and free of speech,
    Or stricken stiff and dumb.
Ah! many a crowd has gathered here
    In the grey morning light,
And many an erring spirit
    Has taken hence its flight;
But never morning dim
    So full of awe drew nigh,
And never man like him
    Stood here before to die.

These were the words that went,
With low, quick breathings blent,
From one to another sent,
    Among the crowds :
'Saw ye not at the trial
    The look that was in his eye,
When he turn'd to his false comrades,
    And said, " I pardon ye ? "
Have ye read that last message
    Unto his people sent ?—
The letter written yestereve,
    His dying testament;
As an emperor to an emperor,
    And yet no scorn nor pride!
Hard task to sign the death-warrant,

With that sheet spread beside!
Ah! feelings strange and dim
Plead in our hearts for him
    More than we dare say.—
    If he had had his way,
    We might have stood to-day
        Like men, and spoken out.—
Nor law nor priest has might
To give unerring light
Whereby to read aright
        His just award :—no doubt,
Murder is deadly sin ;
Yet there was therein
Nothing for him to win
Save what is here ;—
And as it draws so near,
Terrible and clear,
Does it not strange appear
    That one of high estate,
    So gifted and so great,
Without constraint or call,
Should have forsaken all
        Honour'd, and sweet, and dear,
With purpose firm to go
To shame, and death, and woe,
        And none to thank or cheer ?

Has he not given his name
Unto reproach and shame,
Good men's sorrow, proud men's blame;
From history to claim
Only a murderer's fame ?
　　Yea ; has he not besides,
　　　In a whole people's cause,
　　At his own cost defied
　　　Divine and human laws ;
　　The guilt of innocent blood
　　　For ever on his head,
　　To stand before his God,
　　　His hands yet reeking red ?
　　Strange mystery, any heart
　　Could choose such awful part !
　　　Was it madness ?—who can tell ?
Or was it something else
　　We know not of ?—Ah ! well ;
What is it is stronger than fear,—
　　Stronger than Death and Hell ?

Not with the beat of rolling drum,
Or wild fifes wailing, dost thou come,
Tyrannicide, unto thy doom ;
Nothing of sound or light

The spirit to excite
To the stern delight
   Of martyrdom.
The lamps are going out,
   The stars died long ago;—
The death-knell from the chapel,
   Dull, and deep, and slow,—
A sick heart-throb in every stroke,—
   Tolls heavily to and fro.
In the glimmer and gloom of dawning,
   In the winter's mist and chill,
In the people's shiver and shudder,
   Far off, and ghastly still :—
In the serried steel-clad circle,
   Whose grim and glaring eyes
In hungry glee are fix'd to see
   How the assassin dies ;—
With never the face of an old friend
   Standing by thee brave and true ;—
God and thy own heroic heart
   Alone to bear thee through.

PART II.

THE PRISON.

CANDLELIGHT and morning gloom
Struggling in the prison-room,
That dim and desolate chamber, where
   The doomed for their fate prepare.
   A hush'd and solemn company
To-day is gathered there ;
Some standing passionless,
   With faces stern and still,
At their appointed post,
   Hirelings for good or ill ;
Some with clasp'd, quivering hands,
   Now fever-flushed, now pale,
Cold sweat upon their brows,
   Limbs that faint and fail.
Three black and hateful-brow'd,
   Of rude and iron limb,
With cool and practised hands,
   About their labour grim ;
Felon's or martyr's blood,
   It comes alike to them.

Two with deep pious eyes,
Mild with consolation,
That will unshrinking stand,
Strong in Christ, cross in hand,
    Lighting the way.
And in that silent ring
One wild and fluttering—
One with the face of a king
    On his crowning day.

Standing amidst them all,
In that accursed hall,
Fetter'd in helpless thrall,
Vile hands upon thee laid,
In robes of scorn array'd,
    How grand thou art!
Those cold and curious eyes,
Thine aspect stranger-wise
Nor shrinks from nor defies,
    But stands apart;
In unapproached strength,
Resolv'd and fix'd at length.
    There is no human eye,
Nor human aid, intrudes
Into that solitude's
    Heroic agony.

Execution of Felice Orsini.

All clos'd and still,—and yet
The anguish thou hast met
One awful seal has set
 Too visibly.
Since we saw thee last,
What wild change has past,
As the furnace-blast,
 Over thy brow!
In one week that white hair!—
Witness perforce is there
What thou hast had to bear
Of pangs nigh to despair,—
 All over now.
Upon that glorious face
There is little trace
 Of conflicts that have been;
Calm thou standest now,
With grave, majestic brow;
Passive and marble-still;
Through thy frame no thrill
 Nor tremor seen;
No quick flashes rise
From thy deep dark eyes,—
Fathomless there lies
 A veiled soul therein.

This was all thy face betray'd
　　Unto the eyes of men;
What more our hearts may read
　　We cannot tell again.

Yet though thus tranc'd thou seem,
Past thee, as in a dream,
What crowding pictures gleam
　　Out from the past.
All over, and so soon,—
Not forty years are done,[1]
And life for ever gone,—
　　The one die cast!
How fair and sunny shines
That home amid the vines,
　　Far off in Imola;[2]
How soft the day declines
Over the Apennines,
　　Purple afar.
Fearless and full of truth,
What joy it was in youth
　　To feel at every breath
The dawn of manhood breaking,

[1] Orsini was born in 1819.
[2] From nine to thirty years of age Orsini's home was at Imola.

With passionate dreams awaking,
And deep thoughts purpose taking
    For life and death.
That young, full-hearted vow [1]
Of thy whole self, which thou,
Fulfill'd and seal'd, wilt now
    Deliver back to God.
Thy first steps on the way
Which, straight on, till to-day
    Thou in firm faith hast trod;
Those Roman prison-dens accurst,
    Where thou, all slowly withering
In darkness and in chains, didst first
    Measure thy power with suffering,
And felt it equal to the worst,—
    Yea, even to the doom [2]
Of terror and despair that fell
Upon thy youth a freezing knell—
Young Life, and Love, and Hope, farewell !
    Long torture till Death come.
God give patience to the end,
Or some swift succour send,

[1] 'At the age of twenty-two I was admitted a member of the secret societies.'—*Orsini's Memoirs.*

[2] At the age of twenty-five, Orsini was condemned to the galleys for life. The amnesty granted in 1846, by Pius IX., prevented the execution of this sentence.

Or soon call home!
Deliverance at last ;—
When two long years are past,
    The act of grace has come.

1849.

Then arose that dawn sublime,
That short, glowing, glorious time,
The third Rome in her bridal prime ;
When Mazzini's words of fire
    Rang through the halls of Rome,
And the tricolor wav'd out
    Over St. Peter's dome ;
Hark ! the clash of the bells above,
    The people's shouts below
For Rome and the Republic !
    Life is worth having now.
Then, chosen by the people,
    Thy eloquent voice was heard
Thrilling throughout the Capitol,
    Till hearts beneath it stirr'd,
And men rose up to follow thee,
    And thou didst lead them on

Where there was danger to be dar'd,
    Or glory to be won.[1]
Where the dead thickest
    Strew'd the red ground;
Where rattled fastest
    The sharp musket sound,
Where the battle hottest
    Thunder'd around—
Fiercest and foremost
    There wast thou found.
And when the golden time was rent
With lawless deeds and violent,
And others vainly aid had sent,
Thy strong, and just, and fearless hand
Gave peace and safety to the land.[2]
And at the blood-red setting
    Of that scarce hailed star,
When three great armies gather'd,
    Like vultures from afar;
And all around the city bound

---

[1] In June 1849, Orsini led five hundred men to the relief of
Ascoli, besieged by the Neapolitan army.—*Vide* Farini's *History*,
vol. iv.

[2] Ancona was kept in a state of terror by brigands and assassins,
who committed open robbery and murder. Mazzini sent several
commissioners to repress them, who failed to do so. He then sent
Orsini, who immediately restored security.

With narrowing rings of war,
That fiery baptism-tide,
Ye, Romans, side by side,
Did at your posts abide
  Stedfast through all.
How it comes back again,
  That night before the fall !
When the solemn, lighted city
  Up unto God did call;
When the lightning and the thunder
  Burst through the battle's brawl;
When the streets were shaking under
  The hail of bomb and ball,
Till down, in storm asunder,
  Crash'd the defended wall;
When the one look of Mazzini
  Still'd the tumultuous Hall,
And the eyes of Garibaldi
  Were shining over all.

1849 to 1856.

All over !   It was nobly striven;
What use against all earth and heaven?
So, into bitter exile driven,

The strife begins again.[1]
All that story, yet half-told,
Of danger strange and manifold,
Thirst and hunger, heat and cold,
Wanderings wild by field and flood,
Deeds of daring, wounds and blood,
   In peril and in pain.
Often into prisons cast,
Yet no bonds could hold thee fast;
From their hands escap'd and past,
   And forward once again.
Through the snares set in thy path,
Baffling all an empire's wrath;
From city unto city forth,
Calling men to rise and arm,
By the mighty power and charm
Of thy presence and thy name,
Keeping still the spark aflame,
Stirring life where'er they came.
And high hope upbore thee still,
Thy great mission to fulfil;
Nothing might dismay or chill,

---

[1] On the fall of the Roman republic, Orsini retired to Nice. For several years he resided there at intervals; most of his time being spent in organising insurrections in Lombardy and Tuscany. Once during this period he was obliged to take refuge in England.

Till that bitterest stroke of fate
   Thy honour and thy love betray'd—
   The foul and faithless wrong that made
Thy heart and home so desolate.[1]—
Lifelong shadow o'er thee thrown,
   A wound that will not heal :—
Heartsick and reckless, thou art gone
On desperate errand all alone—
Unto none thy purpose shown—
   None bidding thee farewell.
Thou, the hunted and the bann'd,
Into the heart of the strange land,
Darest, with wild purpose plann'd,
To raise it with thy single hand.[2]
Taken at last! and by a foe
Never with life will let thee go :
Too deep and deadly debt they owe;
Thou knowest what to look for now.
All thy sufferings ever told,

---

[1] 'I had been robbed of my happiness, and was yet unrevenged on the destroyer. I shall find him yet.' 'The hope before I die to stand face to face with the traitor who has so foully wronged me.'—*Orsini's Memoirs*.

[2] Orsini, in December 1854, travelled alone through Hungary, Austria, and Transylvania, on a revolutionary mission whose import he never fully revealed.

Heap'd upon thee hundredfold:
Fever, famine, freezing cold,
Their utmost malice wreak'd on thee,
Entreated so despitefully,
The very gaolers wept to see
Thy patience and thy misery.[1]
And thou, as darker clos'd thy fate,
Rising more glorious and great:
Standing before thy judges,
   No friend or witness nigh,
Pallid and feverstricken,
   But the proud light in thine eye—
' Ye have your chains and tortures,
   And I have heart to die.'[2]
The heavy chains, the damp, dark cell,
In the Mantua citadel;
The weary waiting for thy doom,
Alone within that living tomb;
The hope that flash'd on thy despair,
The deed that only thou couldst dare,
That terrible midnight, that wild tale
That froze our cheeks long after pale,

[1] Orsini was arrested at Hermanstadt, in Transylvania. For the terrible sufferings which followed, and which nearly cost him his life, see his *Austrian Dungeons.*

[2] See Orsini's account of his examinations at Mantua.

The dizzy height, the balance frail;
Our hearts within us shrink and quail,
Only thine might never fail;
It reads not like the deeds of men;
God and the angels were with thee then! [1]

1856 to 1858.

Bread of exile once more thine,
Full of bitterness and brine;
Damp, downward-pressing skies,
Cold looks from stranger eyes;
Passionate pleadings thrown away,
Homesick pining day by day,
Strong health fretting to decay;
Till overwearied, overwrought,
How or whence we know not brought,
In fatal hour flash'd this thought,
   Thy strained sense before.
Then the strife, the fever pain,
Fire and frenzy of the brain—

---

[1] See Orsini's account of his marvellous escape from Mantua, March 1856. He then came to England, where he remained till December 1857, endeavouring in vain to excite the Government and the public to interfere in behalf of his country.

Thank God, that worst pain is o'er!
Hatred shall be nevermore.
Thy last perilous journey past,[1]
Thy terrible secret ripening fast;
Mid the giddy whirl and press
   Of this fair city, heard without,
In thy chamber's loneliness,
   By day, with nerved hand and stout,
Working on, and violent death
Hanging over every breath :[2]
Mid the laughter and the light
Of the glittering streets by night,
Moving, as in a dream, apart,
With one stern purpose in thy heart;
The outward calm, the inward fire,
The dark hour drawing nigh and nigher.—
The night of horrors,[3] the wild cry
That through the darkness rent the sky :

[1] Orsini left London for Paris, on his last attempt, December 1857.

[2] The preparation of the bombs used by Orsini was attended with great danger. He undertook the task alone, and was obliged to work with a thermometer always in his hand, to prevent an explosion.

[3] January 14, 1858. Orsini himself was terribly wounded; he was dangerously ill afterwards, of fever, brought on by his bodily and mental sufferings.

On that hour we cannot dwell,
It is too near and terrible.
It is over—let it be,
And all those after days to thee,
Of madness and of agony.
Over, too, with all its glow,
   That last triumphal hour,
When multitudes once more stood hush'd
   Beneath thy spirit's power.[1]
Back to thy cell, whence thou
Wilt come but once more now,
There all alone to hear
Death's footsteps coming near,
Hour by hour more clear.
Death-doom'd, and with the brand
Of murder on thy hand,
To go before God's throne,
   And all those innocent souls
But just before thee gone,
Crying for vengeance there,
Drowning in blood thy prayer,
   Barring thy way.
Mortal anguish, spirit's groan,
All that God and thou alone,

[1] See Orsini's magnificent speech at his trial, February 25, 1858.

Here within these walls, have known.
    And the parting yesterday;
Children's arms, so soft and small,
Round thy neck in passionate thrall,
Where the sharp axe next must fall.
    Ah, let it be !—Not now
Thoughts such as these must must wake
The settled strength to shake
    From that majestic brow.

No man stirred or spake,
None durst the silence break,
    Fall'n on the room.
Thou takest little heed,
As at their work they speed,
    To clothe thee for thy doom;
No sign by which to read
    Thy spirit's light or gloom.
Thou dost not start to feel
The cold touch of the steel,
    As round thy neck the locks
        Are shorn away,
    That the other steel may find
        No hindrance in its way.

Never a motion, never
  A wandering of thine eyes;
The minutes steal away,
And thou hast nought to say:
  How cold and still it is.
Nearer we may not draw;
Hush'd we stand in awe,
  With lingering passionate eyes
Gazing for the last time
Upon that presence sublime,
That in its power and prime
  Is passing away for ever.
The world has seem'd of late
So noble and so great,
All rapt and consecrate
  Unto thy name:
Thou, who the air hast fill'd
  With thy great fame,
Who day by day hast thrill'd
  With words of flame,
For whom in midnights still'd
  Our wild prayers came;
Who even now hast power
To make this fearful hour
  Unutterably dear:—
Too soon it will be past,

We shall have looked our last;
Gulfs unsounded cast
   'Twixt thee and us to-morrow.
     Ah ! rather have thee near
     In all this woe and fear,
     Than be without thee here,
   Alone in sorrow.

He who was join'd with thee,
   And played thee such ill part,
And now thy doom must share,
May not an aspect wear
So lofty in despair,
   But spurreth feverishly
     His sinking heart.
Wild words upon his tongue,
   Cold drops upon his brow;
Thou hast some thought to spare
   For others, even now.
Thou, the slander'd and betray'd,
To the weaker and afraid
Turnest with thy holy aid.
In the depth of thy own struggle and woe
The pardon was given long ago:[1]

---

[1] See Orsini's speech at his trial, February 25.

Passion is over, scorn is past,
And overflowing love at last
   Has all thy soul possest.
'Twas thy last prayer yestereven
His life might be forgiven;
   'My blood alone be given!'[1]
   And now to him addrest,
With an o'ermastering charm,
   On his strain'd ear descend
The grand, grave words, 'Be calm,
   Be calm, my friend!'[2]

Now it is ordered all,
   As the law commands:
The shoes are off thy feet,
   The cords are on thy hands;
The long robes o'er thee cast,
And on thy head at last
   Plac'd the black veil and hood.
Then one lightning streak
Flash'd over eye and cheek.[3]

[1] See Orsini's second letter to the Emperor.

[2] Pierri talked incessantly, with feverish excitement. He was interrupted by Orsini with the words, 'Be calm, my friend, be calm.'

[3] 'When the hood was placed over his head, his face, which hitherto had been calm and impassive, became flushed for a moment, and his eye lighted up.'—*The Times.*

Up in a fervent flood
Rush'd the proud Roman blood:
Before us crown'd he stood
In the glory and the flush
Of the martyr aureole,
And his dark eyes lighted up
At the kindling of his soul;
And on the stedfast lip
Broke forth a smile divine :—
Upon our hearts for ever
That moment's look will shine.

Sorrowful around thee
Together now they crowd;
Thou, their dying prisoner,
All their hearts hast bow'd.[1]
In accents low and broken
The farewell words were spoken;
The farewell back was given
In accents low and still;
Perhaps the thought that moment
Came with a sudden thrill:

[1] 'Orsini spoke little; but when the governor of the prison and
some of the officers approached him, he bade them, in a low tone of
voice, farewell. The turnkey of his cell announced to him in a tone
of regret that his last moment was come. Orsini thanked him for
his sympathy.'

'Better to be as he is
  Than doing a tyrant's will.'

We are ready—all is done;
The hour is all but run;
Beating one by one,
  Loudly the seconds pass.
No heart-sick lingering or delay,
Short and stern is the work to-day.
Thou, full conscious of thy doom,
Hast brav'd Death—and he is come.
Neither doubtful nor afar,
Only the door ajar
Few moments more will bar
  The scaffold from thy gaze.

PART III.

THE SCAFFOLD.

SEVEN strokes toll out the hour,
   Chim'd harsh and slow ;
Now courage ! and God help us all !
   It is time to go.[1]
Ere the last sound has died,
With sudden motion glide
The prison doors aside ;[2]
   Look upward now !
It rises gaunt and grim
Athwart the shadows dim,
Looming in ghastly shape ;
No rescue nor escape.
Forward ! It must be fac'd,
   It is not over yet :
Well that thou hast a hero's heart,
   Or how could this be met ?

---

[1] ' The moment of moving now came, and the Abbé Hugon cried
out, " Courage ! " '

[2] ' The prison clock struck seven : before the last sound died
away, the door leading to the scaffold opened as of itself.'

Over the flinty courtyard
   The dark procession go,
Lighted tapers flickering,
   Funeral shadows throw;
The death-knell tolling, tolling,
   Ever more sad and slow;
And a faint hymn chanted
   Quivering and low;
'Mourir pour la patrie!'
   It is even so.

On to the slaughter led,
Headsman and priest between;
Hands bound behind his back,
Long penance shroud of black,
Bare feet and veiled head,
And a conqueror's proud tread
   Up the steps fifteen.
Via Dolorosa!
   A rude rough way;
Yet mid the mockeries
   Of this dire array
There is a glory on thee
   They cannot take away.
Now most of all we feel,
O Hero! we would kneel

In homage unto thee.—
One went up for this world's weal
  In shame to Calvary.

It seems thou wouldst implore
Leave to speak once more
  In all men's hearing free.[1]
Thou turnest, we can see,
Towards them wistfully,
Those throngs of gazers there,
Who now must witness bear
  For thee to history.
But they are driven back
  Too far for this to be ;
Too mighty mastery lies
In thy voice, in thine eyes ;
Not for enslaved ear
Patriot's last charge to hear :
  So thou must have denial.
Yet fear not, O full heart,
Unread from earth to part ;
Love can those words divine,

---

[1] 'When Orsini appeared on the platform, it could be seen, from the movement of his body and of his head, though covered by the veil, that he was looking out for the crowd, and probably intended addressing them, but they were too far off.'

Needeth nor voice nor sign ;
All our hearts beat with thine
   Through this last trial.
Farewell ! farewell !   The cry
Ariseth far and nigh ;
From the land across the sea,
From thine own Italy,
From souls in slavery
Whom thou didst seek to free,
All the world holds of sympathy
   Is round thee now.
All the world waits to-day
For the tidings that will say,
Thou art pass'd away.
In many a distant home,
   Thou know'st not it may be
Many a tear ere night
   Will fall for thee.
Yes, as thou standest there,
Nations in despair
Lift their eyes to thee,
Wailing passionately—
   'Oh, that it should be thou !
For thy love to us
Perishing, and thus ;—
   Who will save us now ?'

What a deadly stillness,
  What an awful pause ! [1]
Closer and closer o'er us
  The black cloud draws.
In one shuddering silence
  Thousands are bound ;
What a horror of darkness
  Gathers around !
Dizzy our eyes and dim—
  The earth reels to and fro ;
With wildly rattling pulses
  The gasped moments go.
A dark and fearful passage
  We are entering with thee ;
But thy calm aspect lighteth it
  Gloriously.

Thou hast reach'd the place of death—
  Here we must part ;
We may go no further
  With thee, noble heart.
So now blessings, and adieu !
Only One can take thee through ;
Nothing more we can do,

---

[1] 'The prisoners remained exposed upon the platform while an usher read the decree of the Court, condemning them to the death of parricides.'—*Gazette des Tribunaux.*

Save, mid the breathless shiver
Of the death-agony,
Pray our last prayer for thee,
Felice Orsini,
  Once ere we sever:
'God give thee now good speed,
Help in this last great need,
Glory and martyr's meed
  Now and for ever!'

'Miserere, Agnus Dei!'
  The crucifix he kiss'd;[1]
'Thanks, and farewell!' One moment
  The priest's hand he press'd;
Then turn'd and stood in fixed mood,
  To his last work addrest.

Then the veil they rais'd;
But the face on which they gaz'd
  Was calm and glorious still.
Brows that darken'd not nor pal'd,
Eyes that neither quiver'd nor quail'd
  When the first stroke fell.[2]

[1] 'Orsini and Pierri embraced their spiritual attendants, and pressed their lips to the crucifix offered to them.'

[2] 'Pierri was executed first. Orsini was then taken in hand. His veil was raised, and his countenance still betrayed no emotion.

On to the block with steady tread,
Though before him the newly dead,
And comrade's blood gush'd red
    And warm across his way.
' Vive la France!' then he said,
    ' Viva l'Italia!'
Down sunk that noble head;
Shudderings and silence dread;—
    Angels, make way!

        *   *   *   *

Stand still, great world, a moment!
    Fold your hands and pray:
' O God, let all tyranny
    From earth pass away!
Thy kingdom come! and never
    Let there again be need
    Of such o'erwhelming deed,
    Or of such vengeful meed,
    Earth to deliver!'

    Over!—Through all these weeks,
    Hallowing their gloom and pain,

Before he was fastened to the plank, he turned in the direction of the distant crowd, and, it is said, cried, " *Vive la France!*" " *Viva l'Italia!*"'

The shadow of thine agony
　　Over the world has lain,—
A haunting, passionate presence,
　　Beneath whose fixed strain,
We who kept watch with thee have pass'd
　　Through fires of heart and brain.
Now we draw breath, and say,
　　'Thank God!—Well done!'
And out of this Gethsemane
　　At last thy crown is won;
Safe mid the stars for ever,
　　Thou brave, long suffering one!

Thus was thy victory won;
And when the deed was done,
Out went the fiery sun [1]
　　In wrath and fear;
Shadow and tremor fell,
Like the echo of a knell,
By hands invisible
　　Toll'd through the upper air.
All faces in our sight
Pal'd in that awful light
Neither of day nor night:—
　　And all abroad,

[1] The great eclipse of the sun at noon, March 15, 1858, two days after Orsini's execution.

Over the land at noon,
Darkly th' eclipse came on—
For a great soul had gone
    Back unto God.
They laid thee in the prison-yard,
   Coldly and silently;
But the palaces of heaven
   Were hung with black for thee,
And the planets strew'd the pall
Above thee for thy funeral.

So we take leave of thee,
Felice Orsini:
Thy like we shall not see
    On earth again;
Never one century
    Gave two such men.
From thy grave we part
With hush'd and reverent heart,
And comfort in our pain,
Feeling that not in vain
    Such life and death could be;
With hope a coming year
Will yet make all things clear
    By glorious consequence; [1]

[1] The writer holds in firm faith that the Emperor's sudden change
of policy, whence the war in Italy and all the late and present

And we shall wholly see
Through this dark mystery
   Of Providence :
Why one who had stood fast
   In lifelong constancy,
Who had so nobly past
   Through all adversity,
Should have been tried at last
   So strangely, fearfully.
None, knowing thee, can doubt
Thy heart was pure throughout;
   None can thy steps have track'd,
And not felt from the first
The martyrdom the worst
   To thee lay in the *act.*
None hath known, or could know,
The conflict and the woe
Through which thy soul did go
   Ere it gave way.
With brain tost to and fro,
Seething in ebb and flow,
Throbbing and turning so,

glorious events have sprung, was immediately caused by Orsini's
dying letters ; and from the moment of his martyrdom believed that
the salvation of his country would be wrought thereby, though without knowing how. That Orsini's last hours were cheered by the
same faith, we have good reasons for believing. 1860.

Aright thou couldst not tell
Whether from heaven or hell
Those voices round thee fell,
    Ceasing not night or day;
And in that agony,
None helping thee, didst cry,
    As we may deem—
' O, save me from this hour !
Is there no other power
    My nation to redeem ?
Flesh and spirit both
Abhor it, faint and loth ;
Far gladlier would I go
To death by tortures slow,
To dungeons earth below,
All men can make of woe ;—
Their utmost power I know.
Yet, seeing it is so,
And I am call'd thereto,
I may not shrink nor flee
From this now laid on me.
O Mother Italy,
Life, name, and liberty,
And soul, if needs must be,
Were all vow'd unto thee.
    And I have kept that vow

With single heart and true,
All good and evil through,
    As I will keep it now.
For when young life was shining,
And heart with heart entwining,
I chose without repining

    A dark and cheerless road :
Therein these many years,
Through all that nature fears,
In loss, and pain, and tears,

    Straight forward I have trod ;
Till unto me remain'd
Only a name unstain'd ;
Now, that must perish too ;—
There will be still a few

    To judge me tenderly.—
It must be : all I ask,
Is strength for this stern task ;
And for the rest, my God,

    I trust my soul to Thee.
If, in Thy charity,
There is no room for me ;—
If it must be indeed
Thy laws eternal need
That for this loathed deed

    I perish utterly :—

If Thou wilt cast me out,
   I that have clung to Thee
In anguish and in doubt,
   And wrestled fearfully
To know Thy truth ;—yet still,
   Millions for rescue call ;
   It must be,—one for all ;
Here am I,—do Thy will !'

So thy resolve was taken,
And thou, revil'd, forsaken,
Didst bear that cross unshaken
   On through the gates of death.
And past them, at God's feet,
We know that thou didst meet
Award more just and tender
Than any we could render :
   Who knew thy worth as He ?
Upon His mercy cast,
Toil and travail past,
Thou hast found thy home at last,
   And all is well with thee.
The *crime* by death is expiate,
Thou hast bow'd unto thy fate,
Thy place on earth is desolate,
    And it was just :

But the exalted faith,
The hope that triumpheth,
The love prov'd unto death
Tender, and true, and pure,
These cannot but endure ;
And in God's love secure,
Through sorrow-clouds obscure,
      Humbly we trust ;
Thankful that He has given
Another Star to Heaven,
Another name of worth,
To the memories of Earth.

Thou the crown of thorn
With stedfast brows hast worn,—
The world's reproach and scorn,
A heart by wild thoughts torn,
Dungeon depths forlorn,
And this dread judgment-morn :
The utmost thou hast borne,
      And it is o'er :
A name far down to shine,
Rest in the Life Divine,
The red rose crown is thine
      For evermore.

.

BATTLE HYMN FOR GARIBALDI'S BRITISH LEGION.

VOLTURNO, 1860.

GOD bless the cause of Right!
God help us in the fight!
   Guard us from ill!
Soldiers victorious,
High hopes and glorious,
One hero over us,
   God save him still!

His voice went through the land:
Could true hearts idle stand?—
   So we come too.
Red shirts, and English guns,
Strong hands and steady ones,—
England said to her sons,
   ' God go with you!

Bold sons of many lands
With us have shaken hands
    In brotherhood ;
Fast bound for good and ill,
By the same work and will,
By the same breathless thrill
    When first we stood :—

Stood face to face with him,
Stood hand in hand with him,
    Pledged him our faith ;
Saw his smile fade again,
Heard his low voice, and then
Felt we were nobler men
    Henceforth till death.

Now, Garibaldi, then,
Here are thy Englishmen,
    Stout hearts and free;
Take us, thy work to do,
Where thou goest, we go too,
Thou guiding us safe through,
    God guiding thee.

Under those wings divine,
On that high path of thine,
  Forward in might!
With the Archangel's sword,
Bearing to earth abroad
This message of the Lord,
  'Let there be light!'

Heralds of life they find us,
Through all the way behind us
  Peals down the strand
One Hallelujah Chorus;
Christ's own Elected o'er us,
Darkness and doom before us
  Over the land.

Better than life at ease,
Better than gold's increase,
  Doing and daring;
Following his path that lies
Through summer Paradise,
Welcome in all men's eyes,
  His fortunes sharing.

F

Feeling the blood leap free,
Marching to victory,
    Foremost in fight ;
And when the day is won,
Hearing him say ' Well done !'
Standing at set of sun
    Red in the light.

Not all !—we have lost some ;
Speak low !—'twas martyrdom :
    Brave eyes are dim,
When on some battle-eve
Brothers to earth we leave ;—
Sweet hearts at home will grieve,
    God comfort them !

Who next ? We know not yet
Whose sun to-day will set ;
    God's will be done !
Safe in His hands we are,
Who dies in Holy War,
Heaven's angels are not far ;—
    Home, every one !

Now for a glorious day!
Red miles of war array
    Massed firm and ready:
Wave out, sweet tricolor!
Our Chief is gone before,
Far off the first deep roar
    Mutters already.

    *   *   *   *

    *   *   *   *

High in the hottest place
Lightens the Lion-face
    Over the fight.
On, where he leads the way!
Each one as best he may
Trust his own arm to-day,
    God and the Right!

Pulses of cannon-shocks;—
Earth in the thunder rocks,
    Nearer replying.
Hell-fury, fire, and brawl,
One voice rings over all,
That voice whose tender fall
    Comforts the dying.

Rattles the hot hail fast;
This way they come at last,
    Bearing down hither;
On them, through steel and smoke!
Hand to hand, stroke to stroke!
Hurrah! their ranks are broke,
    Charge all together!

Now strike victorious,
Or every man of us
    Here dead will fall!
Viva l'Italia!
All down the line, hurrah!
Darlings in England—ah!
    God bless you all!

TWO SONNETS TO GARIBALDI.

AUGUST 1860.

I.

O LION-FACE, O heart of this world's heart!
  The battle-clouds roll off, the thunders clear,
When face to face we see thee as thou art,
  The face that we have worshipped many a year.
The face that long ago the artist-dreamers
Gave to the kneeling world for the Redeemer's
  In living presence walks the earth abroad,
  And we of this day may behold it near:
High o'er the heat of battle lightening;—
  Or Sabbath mornings, leaning on thy sword,
An hour of rest in conflict, listening
  In silence to the words of Christ thy Lord,
Whose kingdom thou art sent on earth to bring;—
  Or in a sterner presence overawed:—

II.

Standing by sick-beds in the hospitals,
　　Where thy young warriors stricken down are lying,
Watching for thy slow shadow down the walls,
　　And where for one more look of thee the dying
Linger from hour to hour.   The moanings cease
　　Under the yearning pity of thine eyes;
　　And the caressing hand, that fondly lies
On fevered foreheads, smoothes them into peace.
　　And they whose pain is nearly over now
　　　　Lie still, and smile up in their agony
　　　　With angel-eyes of deathless love to thee,
To die and suffer for thy sake content,
For ever thine by that last sacrament,
　　A father's kiss upon their dying brow.

TO THE MEMORY OF FELICE ORSINI.

With the same smile we see thee stand
That lighted up the living land;
Across the starlands thou art come
With thy deep eyes of martyrdom,
As when we saw thee last:—not yet
Can we that hour of doom forget;

That cold March morning when the snows
Were underfoot, and thousands rose
Ere dawn, to see a hero's close;
And thou in silence too didst rise,
And through the darkness gleamed thine eyes,
Led forth unto the sacrifice.

They looked upon thee at the last;—
One smile of lightning flashed and passed,
Across thee from the distance cast:
Since then we have with thanks believed,
Just before Christ thy soul received,
Even then thine anguish was retrieved.

The sun went out,—we could but weep:
No tender hands,—we might not keep
Watch over thee in thy last sleep:
And over thee we sang no psalm,
Lying at last so cold and calm,
Beyond our comfort or our harm.

Ah me ! thou borest heavy doom,
Prisoner white-haired amid the gloom,
That saw the numbered hours consume ;
While in thy brain the phantoms whirled,—
Hearing the voices of the world
In wrath and scorn against thee hurled.

Leaving thine Italy held mute,
There lying, trodden underfoot,
Nor turned to render thee salute ;
Up to the ruthless torturers given,—
Despairing hands stretched out to Heaven,
While deeper in the nails were driven,—
Thou who hadst suffered so, and striven !

Each coward had a stone to throw
Against the mighty lying low ;
None cared to spare thee for thy pains ;
Thy hand, they said, had drawn the reins

More tightly, riveted her chains :—
Thy woe is past, thy work remains.

There standest thou without applause,
Taken on thee a people's cause,
The debt, the doom, of broken laws ;
A cross of death, a crown of thorns,
A brand of blood, a scourge of scorns :—
O wait until the morning dawns !

The dawn is on the mountain's brow,
The prison doors are open now,
Thy work is done,—and where art thou?
In some cold graveyard, dust to dust ;
Spirit to spirit with the just,
Far in some better world we trust.

And knowest thou what thou hast done,
Thou morning-star before the sun,
Who mad'st thyself the victim one?
Knowest thou from that very day,
The salt-flood turned and ebbed away,
The East was quickened with a ray?

If thou hadst lived until this day,
Thou hadst been in the foremost way ;

The name that went down in eclipse,
Had now been hailed by nations' lips;
And thee at Garibaldi's side
The world had known and glorified.

Had this been best?   Ah, who can tell ?
God guardeth his Beloved well,
Quiet beneath their Immortelles.
Thou speakest with thy dreamèd eyes :
'Friend, we who are in Paradise,
Know now our Father is most wise.'

DRAMATIC LYRICS.

VIOLET.

WHEN the buds and blossoms first
In the sudden sunshine burst,
Love came with the sweet spring-tide;
All the earth was glorified,
Violet! my young fair bride.

Violet! with thy young eyes
Tender as the twilight skies;
On thy cheek the first faint rose
That in Aurora's garden blows
When the sunrise overflows.

Fresher and tenderer than the spring;—
On thy finger I slipp'd the ring;
I saw, the old church windows through,
The branches waving to and fro,
All in their first greenness and glow.

Like a lily, bridal-drest,
White and blue violets on thy breast,
White star-flowers upon thy brow,
Violet, I see thee now!
The Angel of First Love wert thou.

Violet, we stood hand in hand,—
The birds were singing through the land,—
Thy little fingers clasp'd in mine,
Thy sweet eyes hidden—I am thine—
Thy long hair round thee a halo-shine.

The sunny world lay fair and wide,
" We gazed out silent, side by side,
And heard on the warm western breeze
A murmur of the early bees
Among the blossoming apple-trees.

And when I brought thee home at night.
The earth was silent with delight ;
The meadows lay all still and green,
Hesperus with passionate sheen
Glittered into thine eyes serene.

But when the Moon of Roses came,
And all the garden was aflame,
All the violets were gone ;—
She died the last, my little one,
Softly she died, at set of sun.

On thy face a smile was set
Like an angel's, Violet ;
Thy hair hung round thee, a bright cloud ;
My lips to thy cold lips I bowed,
And then for anguish cried aloud.

That was a long time ago ;—
Under green grass thou liest low,
And over thee the violets blow ;
And it is harvest time to me,
Who in my April cherished thee.

It has been another world to me
Since then, Violet, wanting thee ;
I have grown in wealth and fame,
My home and haunts are not the same,
I never hear nor speak thy name.

Yet mid the heat and hurry ever,
Like a breath of violets in fever,
See I a sweet spirit glide,
Young and fair and tender-eyed,
Mid soft shadow glorified.

The spring comes ever round again,
With living sunshine and soft rain ;
Then the violets arise,
With their meek and fragrant eyes
Looking at me angel-wise.

Summer airs green garlands bring
In full flush of blossoming ;
Red and white and blue are met ;—
I see them not ;—my eyes are wet,
Thinking of my dead Violet.

Many a maiden passes me
With sunny brow and smile of glee,
Young bright eyes upon me shine ;
Violet, amid them all I pine
For that more beautiful smile of thine !

One hour of Eden in the morn,
At noon the wilderness forlorn ;
Hope waiteth till the sun is set ;—
There will be a summer yet
For thee and me, my Violet.

———◦——

DE PROFUNDIS.

OUT of the voices of the air,
That fill the great world everywhere,
One floated past me, with a sigh
 O'erweighed and broken down :
' The sun shines sadly in the sky,
For I am young, and I must die,
 And die without my crown.
The hope I trusted in, that still
I might be chosen by God's will
Some noble purpose to fulfil,
 Was sent but to befool.
What worthy offering to present
For all the golden talents lent,

For all the earnest striving spent?
With empty hands, I forth am sent,
        That should have been so full.
And what is left, when will is vain,
When every nerve is wild with pain,
And a dull fire is in the brain,
        The thoughts to overrule?
They will not work, they wander on,
All power, but power of suffering, gone :—
And I have missed a greater one,
        And glory these above.
Youth's angel has not come to me ;
I have not known the mystery
Of hand to hand, and heart to heart,
Of life that is not life apart :—
        I have not looked on love :
Before my hour I go to lie
        In a forgotten tomb :
No one will bless me when I die,
        Alone amid the gloom.'
And, weak and broken, many a word
Of deeper anguish yet was heard,
        That moaned and wailed away.
But as I sadly strove to hear,
I heard another voice come near
In accents sweeter and more clear;

' Listen,' it spake, ' I pray :
O dying heart, where'er thou be,
One also stricken speaks to thee ;—
Sometimes an angel says to me
    Words solemn-sweet and calm ;
Upon the fever of my grief
Pouring a music of relief
    Like a mysterious psalm,
Till all my spirit sinks to rest :—
So thou too, howsoe'er distrest
    Or hopeless thou have been,
Take comfort in what comforts me :—
If he has not yet come to thee,
I know that some day thou shalt see
    That angel I have seen.
I cannot tell thee of his face,
Nor promise in what form or place
    He will be at at thy side.
But this I know,—for I have known
All in the wilderness alone,—
When thou art nearing to thy home,
Behold the Bird of God shall come
    Over the waters wide,
To bear the olive to thy soul,
And leave thee from his aureole
    One ray that shall abide;

To tell thee in thy hour of need,
There is a Christ for all, indeed;
He cometh soon, all hearts that bleed
    To bind up tenderly.
Soon shalt thou find thy faith was true,
Thy will fulfilled in works shalt view,
And what thou hadst not strength to do
    Is not required of thee.
Art thou too weak? Dost thou complain
Of the long weariness of pain,
Of agony through nerve and brain,
    Darkly bewildering?
The thorn was twisted round His brow,
Part of His love thou knowest now:
Enter into that hour of woe
Which I beheld, but cannot know,—
    Thank God for suffering!
The depths before thee open on:
Thou canst not know, till hope is gone,
How faith and love may live alone;
Nor till the mind is past control,
The grandeur of the inner soul
    In its own consciousness.
To feel, of life's last hope bereft,
Nothing is lost, for God is left,—
    Yea, this is blessedness!

Ah, yes, my God, my grief grows calm ;
What is there of despair or harm
    While Thou art still Thyself?
In deepest hell I yet will trust,
And worship Thee, O Thou All-Just !
Leave me my love at least they must,
    Because it is myself.—
Words fail—the tears are in my eyes,
Such sweet and solemn thoughts arise
Out of the west, when the sun dies,
    And from the silver sea
Of twilight, o'er the pallid gold,
Glows Hesper forth, as fair as old,
    In diamond royalty.
Be patient but till set of sun,
And whether life be lost or won,
The sweet clear night still cometh on,
    The stars upon her breast.
The shadows pass, the splendours come,
Consoled for evermore at home,
For Love is Lord of all, in whom
    We lose ourselves in rest.'

MANY VOICES.

I WANDERED on out of the town
   Towards the end of May;
The morning sun shone on the spire,
   The market-place was gay;
But the minster-bells were tolling
   Behind me all the way.

    ' What were the minster-bells tolling
      As you came out of the town ? '—
' O sorrow, sorrow, sorrow !
   My love is dead and gone,
It is the merry May-time,
   And I am left alone.'

I passed among the hawthorns,
   Heavy with tinted snow;
There was a flutter of young wings
   Alive in every bough;
All the little birds together
   Were singing loud and low.

'And what were the little birds singing
  In the hawthorns with one breath ? '—
'O my heart is breaking, breaking,
  O young life turned to death !
The sun shines dark upon me,
  And the May air sickeneth.'

I went down through the valley
  To the stream above the mill ;
The cool brown waters glidingly
  Passed by me deep and still ;
The noon-flies flickered in the shade
  Or sunshine at their will.

'And what did the mill-stream murmur
  Silver-sliding to its leap ? '—
'O weary, weary anguish !
  Through the long days to weep !
Down in the quiet waters
  How sweet it is to sleep !'

I crossed the brook to the hayfields
  With meadow-sweet a-scent ;
The tall field daisies smil'd at me
  As underfoot they bent ;
And the long ripe grasses rustled
  Around me as I went.

‘ And what did you hear in the rustling
    Of the field-flowers and the grass ?’—
‘ O stricken-down and broken !
    Down to the dust, alas !
In patience and in lowliness
    The bitterness will pass.’

I went up through the meadows
    To the churchyard on the hill;
And there I found a cross and mound ;
    The mound was bare earth still ;
There I lay down and let my heart
    Break into sobs at will.

‘ And did you hear no whisper,
    There lying, heart to heart ?’—
‘ O love, love, love ! for ever
    My own where’er thou art ;
Be comforted, my darling,
    We are not far apart !’

Then I lay still an hour or more,
    And slept a long sleep there ;
I woke and it was evening,
    The sunset fill’d the air ;
And the sweet church-bells were ringing
    The call to evening prayer.

' And what were the church-bells ringing
  At the time for evening prayer ? '—
' Home, home, home ! in our Father's House,
  And many mansions there.
Christ rose on Easter Sunday,
  And God is everywhere.'

I stood up, and beneath me
  Stretch'd out the golden plain ;
Through the green-shadow'd pastures
  The herds mov'd home again ;
And the full, glorious river
  Unrolling to the main,
Far onward wound and widen'd
  Through leagues of open land ;
Till on the furthest verge gleam'd out
  A line of yellow sand,
And the white evanishing glory
  Of breakers on the strand.

  ' What uttered through the sunset
    The voice of those far seas ? '—
' I could not hear it plainly,
  But listening by degrees,
The choral swell of waters
  Rolled into words like these :
" The Lord shall reign for ever and ever !

His kingdom standeth fast :"
Thanks be to Him for victory!
When darkling faith is past,
When death and hell are conquered,
　　Love is alone at last!"'

———•◦•——

THE IRIS.

With faint steps from a sleepless night,
　　Into the garden forth at noon
I went, and found there no delight,
　　For all the year was out of tune.
The July air was warm, not sweet,
　　There was no sunshine in the land;
Without a sign or sound, to greet,
　　Stood the dark trees on either hand.
Dim lay the heaviness and blight
　　On all the grey oppressive air :—
My heart grew heavier at the sight
　　Of the dull scene that should be fair.

And mournful thoughts about me past,
    Of spring, gone without flowers or sun,
Of summer, that might be the last,
    Of harvest time and nothing done :
Of dreary paths without a clue,
    Of thwarted work and earnest will ;
Of thorny straits gone bleeding through,
    And none the nearer heaven still.
Of all Divine impulses wide
    Of charity and hope, forbidden ;
And duty on the other side—
    Between them both God's will was hidden—
And in the dust gold talents lying,
    Without the strength to take them up ;
Of faith too weak and vague for dying ;
    And that most bitter, hopeless cup,—
Of flesh o'erwrought and wearied brain,
    And nerves unstrung, and all unrest ;
A deep-set ill that turns to pain
    All things that should be pleasantest.

In sorrowful foreboding lost,
    A sudden splendour caught my eyes
From tangled flower-beds, where it crost
    The green, light leaf-cloud, sunbeam-wise.

A gorgeous Iris I saw stand,
　　Arrayed in deep and dusky flame ;
Like rainbows to a rainy land,
　　Its marvel-glory to me came.
It spoke like sunlight unto me,
　　It thrilled me with an arrowy fire
Of answer to the mystery
　　And pining waste of my desire :
' God can work without thee, sad heart !
　　Thy weakness will not stay the world;
Nor worlds, in order, each apart,
　　Through all the spiral orbits curled.
One great good Will is Love and Life ;
　　It ruleth on, it triumphs still,
It works its own best ends through strife, ,
　　Through mystery and seeming ill.
What thou hast been ordained to be,
　　Is well ordained, and must be so :
If the good never come to thee,
　　Some better purpose thou shalt know.
'Tis blessedness to *do* God's will,
　　Already if thou canst discern,—
That same to *suffer*, dark and still,
　　May be the lesson yet to learn.'

THE CHILDREN.

FATHER and mother, many a year
In rain and sunshine we have lived here,
    And the children—
And now that the winter days are come,
We wait and rest in our own old home ;
    But where are the children ?

All so young, in the times of old
Not a lamb was missing from our fold,
    And the children—
God's ways are narrow, the world is wide,
I would have guarded them at my side ;
    But where are the children ?

We walk to the house of God alone,
From the last year's nest the birds have flown,
    And the children.—
Alone by the silent hearth we sit,
The chambers are ready, the fires are lit;
    But where are the children ?

My life is failing, my hair is grey,
I have seen the old years pass away,
    And the children—
My steps are feeble, my voice is low,
I am longing to bless you ere I go ;
    But where are the children ?

I had a dream of another home ;
I thought when He called us I should come,
    And the children—
And say, at the feet of Our Father in Heaven
Here am I, with those Thou hast given :—
    But where are the children ?

The day of the Lord is coming on ;
We shall meet again before God's throne,
    And the children—
Father and Mother, we trust, shall stand
Together then at God's right hand :—
    But where are the children ?

ARCTIC CHRISTMAS.

I HAD a garden down in the south,
  Snowed with myrtle, rosy with vine.
If it had come by prophet's mouth,
  That hard message, with power and sign,
'Get thee hence, and leave thy garden!'
I should have held back, crying, 'Pardon!
  Too much—I cannot. Is it not mine?'

So, without escape or warning,
  Came an angel with face of wrath,
Laid my Eden waste in the morning,
  Shut the gates and led me forth;
Set flaming swords against each comer;
From my paradise of summer
  Drove me out into the north.

All alone, cut off returning,
  Winter and wilderness everywhere;
Looking back with a hopeless yearning.
  The trees were rocking black and bare;

The damp dead leaves were strewing the way,
The chill rain began to pour through the grey,
    And forward I must fare.

Through the great cities, perished with hunger ;—
    The bare gaunt workshops had ceased their din.
Not a fire glowed from the windows longer,
    Through the empty streets the rain drove thin.
The people were in ; I met no faces,—
Waiting silent in their places
    Till the fever should begin.

Northwards still, and the sleet came flying
    With the whistling wind, so eerily ;
Beside me long flat sands were lying,
    Shimmering out to a far cold sea ;
Where the flocks of stormy sea-birds hover,
Nothing else for the sky to cover
    But the salt sand wastes and me.

Jagged white spectres nodded their heads,
    Dead-white against the smoke-black sky,
Where the awful mountain wilderness spreads
    In a cloudy winter-world on high ;
Under their giant horror, then,
The ghastly darkness of day began
    In freezing twilight to die.

Falling ever thicklier and stillier,
   Lay the snow o'er the Arctic girth ;
Ice-shapes looming stonier and chillier
   Over the desolate field and firth.
Numb as a corpse the earth was lying,
All things were dead, and I was dying ;—
   Was there ever a summer on earth ?

Dead I lay there, dead in the snow,
   Wrapped in God's last merciful calm,
Till the vision of the days ago
   Stole around me with Eden balm ;
And I saw her lying clothed in white,
Lovely as on our marriage night,
   Closed eyes and folded palm.

O blessèd vision, that held me fast,
   Moments or years, in a rapt suspense !
What was the perished sunshine past,
   And the dark way's pains, for this recompense ?
Heart of home in the world-wide waste ;—
One motion forward, and all was past
   In vanishing darkness hence.

I wept such tears as I had not wept
   Before, in a twice-dealt agony ;
Till lustrous at last before me stept

H

And stood on the snow a Child; and He
Spake unto me, ' Lo ! I am born ;
Wherefore, then, dost thou weep, and mourn
 The dead whom I keep for thee ? '

All are gone as I wake at home—
 The desolate home, that once was gay ;
The bells are ringing, for Christ is come,
 ' Christ is born ! ' in the air they say;
Not to the gardens of earthly delight,
Into the winter, into the night,
 The Lord is born to-day.

Time to rise ! The sunshine has perished,
 The air is chill and the skies are grey ;
The poor to be fed, and the weak to be cherished,
 And the lost to be rescued, where are they ?
' With you always ; ' though heart be breaking,
Let it work and keep down the aching ;
 Christ will take care of it some day.

THE FALL OF THE LEAF.

I LAY this charge upon you,
　My truest, tenderest friend,
That to these words, when I am dead,
　You for my sake attend.

I have not seen you for so long,
　In all my grief and pain ;
And now I think I never
　Shall see your face again.

For I am far in stranger-land,
　And sinking heart and flesh ;
The rain streams down my lattice,
　My tears stream down afresh.

I have not one to turn to,
  God has forsaken me quite;
And I am going all alone
  Into the empty night.

I never had a tender hand
  Of mother, sister, friend,
About me in my sicknesses;
  But when my life shall end,

Oh, if you can, come to me then,
  Kiss me before I die;
There will be no one at that hour
  Will want you so much as I.

So for the last time, dearest,
  Bear with me, and forgive
A sick child's foolish fancies,
  Who has not long to live.

I give you this last trouble
  And labour for my sakè,
That with your own hands, dearest,
  You shall my white robe make.

All straightly gathered to the throat,
   And worked with simple bands
Of delicate ruffled edging
   Around the neck and hands.

Let it be fine and delicate,
   Because I once would lie
Lovely and tender to behold
   Unto a loving eye.

And if my hair be still as long
   And bright as it is now ;
Smooth back the tresses either side,
   And lay them from my brow,

And let them flow down over me
   In long, loose, shining fold,
As they do in these desolate nights,
   Wrapping me from the cold.

And then take from my finger
   The pearl ring that I wear,
And place it over your wedding-ring,
   And keep it always there.

Lay in my hands no token
　Of laurel or of palm ;
Will it not be enough for me
　Not victory, but calm ?

Lay them together on my breast,
　There let them folded lie,
As one whose best deed was a prayer,
　Whose life was but a cry.

And once at last smooth over
　My forehead with your hand ;
I shall wish to be alive again
　To feel it and understand.

Here I lie sobbing in the dark,
　Stretching out my hands in vain ;
Knowing I never can find yours
　To clasp and kiss again.

Oh, will you not be sorrowful ?
　Alas ! I know you will.
Sweetest, if I could comfort you,
　I would be living still.

And once before you leave me,
 Kiss me that I may rest ;
And then when it comes over you,
 I, too, am crown'd and blest,

Kneel down to God our Father,
 And say, if thou canst say,
' He bringeth the outcasts home again,
 And those that are out of the way.'

 * * * * *

And I will not be buried here
 Among the long dank grass,
And shiver of the falling leaves,
 Where only strangers pass.

But there, where I have lived my life,
 And dreamed my dreams, and sung,
And wandered, through my fitful youth,
 The well-known ways among.

There is a churchyard off the road,
 Down to the stream inclin'd,
Crowded with stones and shapes in front,
 But quieter behind.

A little while ago it was
  A fair and quiet spot ;
It may be but a crowded place,
  When I shall be forgot.

There, looking for the minnows,
  The town-bred children play,
The only witnesses to them
  Of sweet streams far away.

And I know every step of the way
  That leads from it to your door ;
I have walked there so often,
  As I shall walk no more.

There let me be laid lowly
  Where the short grass grows green :
No stone, no token—who will care
  For what I might have been ?

Only you will come there sometimes,
  The dearest that I had ;
And think of me in the sunshine,
  And my spirit will be glad.

And perhaps on Easter Sunday,
   When sweet winds begin to blow ;
When the pear-trees in the valley
   Are white with blossom-snow,

My father may come there slowly,
   And hear no other sound
But the little birds all singing,
   And the young leaves bursting round,

And my voice miss'd for ever—
   And feel as the shadows fall,
That I cannot walk back home with him,
   Nor meet him in the hall :

And dim through tears behold me,
   A sweeter, happier child ;
At last no shadow in the home
   Where all are reconcil'd.

MISCELLANEOUS.

A WEEK IN JULY.

SUNDAY.

THE lilies stood out in the sun
    Against the glossy laurel-green,
    And many a summer-folded screen
Of foliage, woodbine-overrun.

The house behind a shadow threw
    Cool on the new-mown churchyard sward,
    On trailing ivy, darkly starr'd,
And the low hedge of shining yew.

They full in front, a dazzling mark,
    O'erflowed the garden with their light ;
    When the church clock struck twelve last night
I saw them shining through the dark.

I think that Christ's own hand did mould
    The lily, when the rest had been
    Fashioned by angels, as serene
The sixth day's dawn began to unfold

O'er solitary Eden lawns,
    Waiting their crown amidst the hush ;
    While darted through the green the flush
Of the first rose, without the thorns.

      *   *   *   *   *

      *   *   *   *   *

MONDAY.

UNDER a bush of barberries
    That seemed to ripen as I lay,
    Turning to crimson, as the day
Mounted to noon through glowing skies.—

Up in the blue my eyes were lost,
    High overhead, in vivid light,
    Ceaseless the swallows' breasts of white
Forwards and backwards flash'd and crost.

The garden flowers rose dazzlingly
 Beside the lawn, the walks among ;
 The myriad-blossomed roses hung
An arch in air against the sky.

Beneath me the green valley fell ;
 And past the brook, the lone hillside
 Of moor and copse, and pasture wide,
In the broad sunshine stretched as well.

The sloping turf whereon I lay,
 Starr'd with dry golden flowers, was warm
 Unto my hand ; no voice or form
Broke the still glory of the day.

TUESDAY.

THREE years he lies on his low bed,
 In his dark chamber night and day,
 From all life-converse laid away,
The naked thatch above his head.

The little window far behind
 With one straight ray across the gloom
 Makes groping twilight in the room ;
For him he might as well be blind.

Yet sweetly the small window frame
    The heathy hill-side picture sets,
    Sparkling with tiny rivulets,
In May a sheet of spiky flame.

And a hoar apple orchard placed
    Close by, through all the year in suit
    Swings boughs of bloom and leaf and fruit
In the green garden off the waste.

But he, that old man, cannot turn
    Nor move, and lies, his face away
    From what few glimpses of the day
Another prisoner might discern.

To narrowest deprivation tied,
    He murmurs never, still content
    To take the hours as God hath sent,
In patience meek and dignified.

Thus, through a long-drawn living death
    He keeps his manhood true and whole,
    The peace of heaven within his soul,
In utmost simpleness of faith.

So, mindful how forlorn he lay,
 I brought a mirror in my hand,
 That he might once more understand
By sense, the long-lost light of day.

By careful measure of the light
 I held and moved it till there came
 The corner of the window frame
Reflected straight before his sight.

Till, broken first and fluttering,
 Caught in the mirror came and went
 'Mid the unshapely dark long-pent,
A blue ethereal glimmering;

Then held there, settled bright and calm,—
 The sky! the sky! the heavens above!
 The blue great depths of light and love:
The three years had not done them harm.

The same young skies of other years!
 And bending half across, one bough
 Of apple leaves, drawn clearly, now
Against the glowing space appears.

1

Far up the sky shone on between :
    A low and rustling wind we heard,
    And in the mirror the leaves stirred,
Each sweet and wondrous leaf of green.

His dim eyes lightened to the blue,
    He gazed, and gazed, and speechless still
    He scarcely breathed, to gaze his fill
On the old world brought back to view.

' I see the sky and leaves again ! '
    At last he said, and happy lay :
    A few square inches of the day
Such deep contentment may contain !

WEDNESDAY.

I went out when the day grew cool,
    An hour from sunset, far and free
    To gather wild flowers, and with me
Two orphan children from the school.

We went down through the elm tree lane,
    Till by the mill we crost the brook,
    And past the shady hollow took
The other side our way again,

A Week in July.

Up the steep lane, where the tall hedge
  With honeysuckle down was weighed
  O'er ferns and foxgloves half in shade,
Until we came out on the edge

Of the great moorland, stretching brown,
  O'er which to me there ever dwells
  The mystery as of magic spells,
And hoar enchanted glow at noon.

But now at sunset a wild light
  Flared on the crimson tracts of heath;
  And the long grasses wav'd beneath
A melancholy breeze's flight.

We went on heaping ferns and flowers,
  Blush-tinted bells and waxen white
  Of heath, and sundews exquisite,
Sparkled all o'er with fairy showers.

The golden rods of asphodel
  Shook, as with firm light steps we trod
  O'er the deep moss and spongy sod
Strewed with the small bog-pimpernel.

We talked of country lore, of ferns
    With mystic letters stamped inside,
    Of hard-found nests where lapwings hide
Their eggs amid the heath, in turns.

We past the dripping woodland cleft,
    Where hanging ferns clos'd overhead
    On grey rocks, and the streamlet's bed
Rough passage to the thicket left.

We passed the level of brown moss,
    Above the borders of the wood,
    Lying in breezy solitude,
With sunset shadows stretched across;

Where on June evenings I have found
    That fair mysterious flower [1] upright
    And single-stalked, in green and white
Springing enchanted from the ground;

A haunted, shadowy gleaming flower,
    Scentless by day, but through the gloom
    Floated in rapturous perfume
Of orange-blossom, one dream-hour.

[1] The Butterfly Orchis.

Past the wild hollow, craterlike,
    I wander'd half a summer's day
    To find, where th' rare bog-bean in May
Throws up a rosy fringèd spike

From leafage smooth and broad, and makes
    A fairy floating island, plac'd
    In the grey centre of the waste:
And past the shallow pools and lakes

Where the tall crested birds by day
    Stalk to and fro and dip their heads;
    And where the cotton grass outspreads
White silken streamers in array.

Then downward turning, we came past
    The lone grey cottage on the moor,
    In its green orchard nook secure,
Homelike and shelter'd from the blast;

With the young ash trees grouping near;
    Where smoothest greensward from the door,
    Sprinkled with daisies, spreads before,
And a tiny brooklet, silver clear,

All wreath'd with thick forget-me-not,
　　And golden spearwort with its leaves
　　Pointed in flowing, threads and cleaves
Its light way through the open spot.

The Irish boy, with his fair brow
　　And wide blue eyes, a child whose look
　　Itself all hearts in pleasure took
To see his smile, was standing now

Triumphant. with his hands o'erfull
　　Of white silk plumes, amid the moss;
　　His radiant face and hair across
Flushed the wild sunset, beautiful.

The other with his eyes of love
　　Walk'd close by me, and on my face
　　He gaz'd as on a charmèd place,
And hardly from my side would move.

And now the twilight had begun
　　To darken over hill and dale;
　　Across the valley glimmer'd pale
Lights from low windows, one by one.

Ah, there stood homes, tho' bare and poor!
 The lapwings rose disturb'd, and screamed
 Above our heads, the night-moths gleamed.
And we were out upon the moor.

THURSDAY.

Upon a winding height, our way,
 With low wood rolling to its base;
 And far below, for miles to trace,
Clear at our feet the valley lay

In cool delicious depths of green,
 And evening stillness of repose—
 In one clear light of golden-rose
The distant West glow'd on serene:

But over lowlands near at hand
 The very air was dewy-green;
 The waters wander'd through a scene
The very heart of summer-land.

The fresh and feathery elm-trees stood
 The silent meadow-grass above;
 The quiet shadows did not move
Through all the lovely solitude.

A green sweet Eden, wild and low
    Winding far off amid the hills;
    For ever cool'd by hidden rills,
Under the leafage trickling slow.

The great white owls, with floating wings,
    Over the twilight meadows hung
    In the soft, silent air, and swung
Across with sudden glimmerings.

Then, downward winding, we drew near
    The rocky orchard, rising steep,
    Standing in thick grass ankle-deep,
With bursting springs descending clear,

Meeting in one white network all,
    Foaming and cool, round beds of stone
    With golden saxifrage o'ergrown,
And pour'd in one wild waterfall.

FRIDAY.

LIGHT summer clouds sail'd on aloft;
    The shadows of the afternoon
    Were slanting over mound and stone,
In the green churchyard, warm and soft.

I sat beneath a cedar tree,
    Around me golden disks of flowers,
    Long-stalked, through all the noon-day hours
Had floated on a deep green sea;

But now were closing, folded green,
    Lost in the long grass, lately mown,
    Which, now once more luxuriant grown,
An emerald setting lay between

The velvet-dark of cypresses
    And young, fair-shooting deodars;
    On the low steps the ivy-stars
Clung in a tangled wilderness.

The ancient church-tower, golden-hoar,
　　Stood up into the summer air
　　Against the vivid blue, in bare
And stedfast service evermore,

Fronting the sun, while round and round
　　The jackdaws wheel'd with sudden cries,
　　And swallows shot into the skies
And back again without a sound.

The white and yellow butterflies
　　Flutter'd low down and skimm'd the grass;
　　I saw their waving dances pass
In airy light before my eyes;

Sitting beneath the canopy
　　Of cedar branches spreading low;
　　While, rapture-beautiful and slow,
The golden hours mov'd thro' the sky.

SATURDAY.

THE sun shone on the village street:
    The low doors, standing open, made
    In the grey walls retreats of shade,
Amid the glowing summer heat.

Aloft against the azure light
    The slender grasses ripe and tall
    Stood tufted on the rough stone wall
Mellowed with lichens warm and bright.

Low, thatched old gables, overgrown
    With ivy, caught the morning lights;
    By shining, silvery pigeon flights
Sometimes in soft, swift shadow thrown.

The Gothic buildings of the school
    Stood open wide, with many a one
    Coming and going in the sun,
Over against the churchyard cool.

In the arched doorways, with the sky
    Behind them through another door,
    Stood simple forms of girls, before
They mov'd to greet us going by.

Shelter'd all round, but hoar with age
    Still on the hill-side lay the church;
    And with the cross above the porch,
The ivy-mantled parsonage.

All round, bright life to service given,
    Voices of youth, and looks of bloom,
    Blessing of love, and peace of home,
And over all the smile of heaven.

THE LIGHT OF THE WORLD.

THE pearly purple clearness
  Of heaven's gates at morn
Through closèd eyelids interwove
  With dreamings of the dawn ;
And down the gleaming shadowy ways,
  In long low light withdrawn,
I saw the young hours brightening back
  Far off where 1 was born ;
All peach and apple blossom,
  With promise and delight,
A heaven of cloudless sun by day,
  And golden stars by night.
Bright lay the way before me,
  And brighter to its close,
The farther future ever lit
  With deeper tints of rose ;
Till where, amid the western heaven,
  The glory overflows.
Now, standing at that western gate,
  Looking back whence I came,

Those long grey desert pathways
  Could never be the same—
Behind me all in shadow,
  Before me all aflame.

Rose the ideas of youth again,
  With grand and glorious eyes,
The visions of immortal things
  And works that should arise.
Large talents feeling for the air,
  Life bursting into song ;
The keen and dauntless spirit,
  In hope and purpose strong,
For labour in the vineyard,
  Or battle against wrong :
Deep, deep into the morning
  Dreaming, for life was long.
Ah, full and fair the shoots of spring
  Waved over all the plain ;
Now come the harvest angels -
  Where is the golden grain ?
O Life, of all thy working day,
  Does only this remain ?
Of torn and tangled fragments,
  Not one without a stain.

The dead stood up before me
　　Once more, as they had been,
My own to love and comfort,
　　In daily dearness seen;
Sweet faces that all silently
　　With my wild moods had pleaded,
Whose unreproachful sadness
　　Fell on me then unheeded;
Who looked to me for sunshine,
　　And found not what they needed.
'Come back to me one little hour,
　　And I will tend you so;
Oh, if you were but mine again,
　　I would not let you go;
If I had known you would have died!
　　Too late, too late I know.'

The cold hand shook not in my tears,
　　No eyelid flushed or fell;
They spoke in clear calm voices,
　　' We rest, and we are well;
All is forgiven long ago;—
　　With thee we may not dwell.'
They passed away and out of sight
　　Ere I could say farewell.

And every beggar in the street
　　I ever had passed by,
'O stay, that I may help you now!'
　　But they made no reply;
Then I knew what it was to beg,
　　And no man heed my cry;
I wept aloud for anguish,
　　None stopped to ask me why;

And then I saw One standing
　　In the December night,
With bare feet on the frozen ground,
　　And in His hand a light.
The wondrous face was turned this way,
　　Full in the lantern shine;
Under the thorns the deep eyes looked
　　Their message into mine,
As then He knocked and waited
　　Before a close-shut door,
With withered red-leaved creepers
　　And tall dry weeds grown o'er;
No stir, no answer from within,
　　Yet knocking evermore.
Ah! I remember now how long
　　I turned away and slept,

While under the cold stars all night
   His patient watch He kept,
Though all the yearning angels
   Were wearied out and wept.
' Here am I ; nor will I depart
   Until Thou let me in ;
The heavens are far behind me,
   One human soul to win ;
That thou mayest know My mercy
   Is greater than thy sin.'

' Light of the World ! I know thee now,
   That might have been my own ;
And I have chosen darkness :
   Now darkness cometh on,
And it is I must call in vain ;
   The Lord of Light is gone.'
Then, in despair, unto the winds
   The door I opened wide ;
And lo ! the same as ever,
   That bright One stood beside,
With the same smile upon Thy face,
   O Crownèd, Crucified,
As when Thy hand stretched o'er the sea
   To Peter, who denied.

K

I sank in bitter weeping
　Beside the open door—
' O good Lord, give me back one hour
　Of all that went before ! '
. I heard a deep voice tolling,
　' Nevermore, nevermore ! '
On it went echoing under,
　Down to the gates of hell ;
Helpless and broken-hearted,
　Into Christ's arms I fell ;
I heard the angels saying,
　' He doeth all things well.'

THE INDIAN SUMMER.

THE pale-blue heaven unclouded stays
　From day to day, and now indeed
The fairest of October days,
　By the broad reaches of the Tweed,
With softest sunshine fills the band
　Of silver-purple liquid light,
　In the noon silence, Sabbath bright,
Unrolling through the Autumn land.

Half-stripped, the wooded banks lift high
  A carven lacework of grey boughs,
Soft brown and gold against the sky ;
  And here and there full-gloried glows
Some crown the spoiler has passed by,
  In crimsoned, passionate repose,
  Waiting until the north wind blows,—
  A pale flower ripened to a rose,
' One last rich hour before I die ! '

Not long ago, all overgrown,
The heavy-foliaged bank shelved down,
At noonday laid in twilight brown ;
When, as the sunbeams slanted through,
A million dancing emeralds threw
  A glowworm sparkle back again.
Now bright in sunshine everywhere
The shining grey-ash stems are bare,
  And thinly overspread
By delicately figured shade,
In mottled motion on them laid
  From the pale witch-elms overhead,
    Still hanging forth their wreath ;—
Light crossed with shade, for shade with light ;—
And withered leaves to-day are bright ;

Half of them on the ground are spread,
Mosaic pavement gold and red,
And some still flutter overhead,
And some are borne along the stream,
And all the air is full of them,
    Dancing away to death.

Now after hoping long and vain,
The summer is come back again,
With angel eyes and brow serene,
To show us what she might have been ;
All the regrets she cannot speak,
In the flushed silence of her cheek,
And the child-tender eyelids meek
    In their translucent fall.
We watched her coming from the south
With joyous welcome to her youth ;
The suffering, worn by sickness, blest
The angel that should give them rest ;
    She came and mocked us all.
For she was gloomy, cold, and wild,
A fitful, weeping, passionate child,
Uncertain even when she smiled ;
    But that is over now ;
The waywardness and grief are past,
She has a tender heart at last.

She comes to take farewell to-day,
So beautiful, we can but say
' With us a little longer stay ! '
    But doom is on her brow.

All lovingly and lingeringly
Flooded in golden ecstasy
Flows the great river's heart, as he
Through the clear silence, mellow-warm,
Knows the approaching of her form ;
    Her robes around her dim ;
Faint floating veils the light shines through
Tinged airily with mountain blue
    As she comes down to him ;—
Down soft and slow through sunlit space,—
She hovers o'er him face to face,
Her warm arms spreading to embrace ;
Her spirit eyes are close to him,
Her sweet eyes that will soon be dim ;
He feels her lips a moment prest,
Her golden hair upon his breast,
And an unutterable rest
    Circling through all his spirit thrills,
And into motion quietest
    The gliding current stills.

A golden haze on Cheviot lies,
  And it is midday now—he knows
That when this day in sunset dies
  She will go from him ; and the snows
Will bury her upon the hills,
  And winter winds howl over her.
So this last day for him she fills
  For ever lovelier.

The soft wind and the yellow leaves
Are having their last dance together,
Up and down, an oriole feather.
'O life, and love, and summer weather !
Is this our parting ?'   Even so :
A little gust of wind, and lo,
A flight of golden butterflies
  In slow and airy quiver
Winged downwards, and each dead leaf lies
  Floated along the river.
And over them the lost wind sighs,
  They lying calm for ever.

MIDNIGHT ON CALVARY.

THE night was come after the day
  Of the great Agony,
When Peter from Jerusalem
  Went up to Calvary.

Alone and silently he passed
  Out of the eastern gate,
Above all others on the earth
  Stricken and desolate.

The nightingales sang not that night,
  For Christ lay dead on earth ;
The olive-leaves stayed whispering
  As Peter wandered forth.

The moon came slowly up the east,
  A glittering, large full moon ;
And the dumb land grew clearer :
  Midnight was coming soon.—

The Master was not watching
   Up on the hills in prayer.—
He stood still in the shiver
   And darkness of despair.

He lifted up his eyes, as one
   That wakens from a swoon,
And he saw the three gaunt crosses
   Stand black against the moon.

Apace he hurried up the hill
   Where, a few hours ago,
Under the burning sunshine,
   Christ had gone up so slow.

On the one side lay Golgotha,
   Trodden and heaped around ;
On the other side all quiet,
   The rocky Garden ground.

The moonlight glanced across the flowers,
   And struck the broad white stone,
The door of that new sepulchre
   Where Christ was laid alone.

Midnight on Calvary.

Down stricken to his knees he fell,
   And sobbing out aloud,
Where John had stood all stedfast,
   His face to earth he bowed.

'O Master, blessed Master !
   Is this the end of all ?
And was that our last parting
   This morning, in the hall ?

'One look straight through the darkness
   Ever against me cries ;
O silent Lord, I cannot bear
   The sorrow of Thine eyes !

'Betrayed, forsaken, slandered,
   In bitterest need and woe ;
I was not with Thee here, Lord ;—
   Ah ! that it should be so !

'We know not whither Thou art gone,
   We do not know the way ;
All light, and hope, and comfort,
   Are gone from earth to-day.

' Left all alone, and in the dark,
    If I had been more wise,
I might have been this very hour
    With Thee in Paradise.

' O Lord, have pity on me now,
    That my heart may not break
Before I have done or suffered
    Aught worthy for Thy sake.'

     *   *   *   *

First seen of Mary Magdalene,
    Of Peter after next ;—
The words that then were spoken
    Are written in no text.

THE LADY'S STEPS.

READY for her flight she stands.
With her jewels in her hands ;
She is hostage for her lord ;
Trusting to his monarch's word,
He has sheathed his rebel sword,
Waiting for the law's award
    In his Buchan tower.
She has overheard it said,
How his promise is betrayed,
How a price is on his head ;
If he be not warned to-night,
Murder comes with morning light ;—
    She will fly this hour.

From the foemen's bounds secure,
Past with stealthy step and sure,
    Mute and holding breath ;—
A wild day's journey lies before
She can see her own home more ;

Over moss and moor, the track
Leads through desolate sheep-walks back,
Buchan wastes and forests black,
    A race for life or death.

Evening fell all wild and red,
Storm clouds gathered overhead ;
Faster through the gloom she sped,
    Heard the plover cry,
Heard, where moorland waters meet,
On the hills the last lamb bleat ;
Crushed the thorns against her feet,
Past her blew the slanting sleet,
On her shoulders low boughs beat ;—
Through the shadows firm and fleet
    That white form went by.

Through the low air comes a stir,
Near and nearer after her ;
Armèd horsemen, pricking spur,
Flash into the landscape dim,
Death to her and death to him ;
She is straining every limb
    O'er the open ground.
The low wall before her lay,
With a leap she cleared the way

The Lady's Steps.

O'er the stones, and there they stay :
' The lady's steps ' unto this day
    By the garden bound.

Ah ! for help when need is most !
Help is none, and all is lost.
In a ring of flashing swords,
No time is now for many words.
Standing stately by the brook,
Back from her brows the hair she shook ;
In one rapid moment took
Round on every face a look,
    Dauntless spoke aloud—
' That great day is coming, when
God shall judge the sons of men ;
I shall know you all again
When we meet before Him then.'
Eyed the steel without a frown,
Proudly spoke, and then knelt down
    Meekly unto God.

To the lake the burn ran red ;
Moaning voices, it is said,
    Haunt the place at fall of day ;
Through the reeds the low winds sigh,
And the wildfowl's wailing cry

Rings a curfew in reply ;
While, with one long note, on high
The straight black thread of rooks sails by,
Stretching to the farthest sky
On their homeward way.

———◆———

FRITZ AND WILHELMINA.

Two fair children, sister and brother,
King's son and daughter, clinging to each other,
Fritz and Wilhelmina.

He high of heart, and strong and stout of will,
She bright and brave, and a spirit all athrill,
Fritz and Wilhelmina.

Prince and princess truly, but no princely life, God knows,
Hard fare and harder words, bonds and mocks and blows,
Fritz and Wilhelmina.

Rough times are coming—we will cling together,
Fast heart to heart through all the stormy weather,
          Fritz and Wilhelmina.

Through the blinding darkness, through the pelting storm,
Hold fast together, keep your young hearts warm,
          Fritz and Wilhelmina.

Heavier crashing thunderclouds, blackening almost unto
    death,
The king's son is in prison, the king's daughter lan-
    guisheth,
          Fritz and Wilhelmina.

Parted, sister and brother, dark times are come indeed,
Now must we pray for each other in our need,
          Fritz and Wilhelmina.

Face to face once more, ere the world sunders you twain,
Out of your youth's prison, changed, ye meet again,
          Fritz and Wilhelmina.

He henceforth a man and silent, a ruler among men,
Great to be called, but never the free in heart again,
          Fritz and Wilhelmina.

She to be a royal mother, a sweet star in the land,
One whom all could love and few could understand,
      Fritz and Wilhelmina.

Children, were they so bitter. the troubles of your youth.
When ye were all each other's in tenderness and truth,
      Fritz and Wilhelmina ?

Worse things the age will bring you, when ye shall be
   apart,
Cold faith, and broken reeds. and hardening of the heart,
      Fritz and Wilhelmina.

Now perhaps, the long day over of earthly toil and pain,
In the Palace Gardens ye are young again,
      Fritz and Wilhelmina.

NORTH WINDS.

THE March winds rave between the hills,
Cold run the steel-blue shining rills,
Through the wide void a wailing shrills.

The sun is high at equinox,
The cold blast the pale sunshine mocks,
Helpless the giddy rookery rocks.

Ice gathers on the scarce-loos'd flood,
The sap stands still within the bud,
Chill slackens soon the heart's young blood.

The far heights start out one by one,
Down the hill-sides cloud-shadows run
Across the cold glare of the sun.

The long marsh in the windy vale
With sedges lightens and turns pale,
Pointed one way before the gale.

There were some flowers short time ago,—
When the wind falls will come the snow;
O foolish flowers, why did ye blow?

All wan and dazzling overhead
The Arctic flood is tost and spread :—
Methinks the Spring itself is dead.

DWELLERS IN PARADISE.

THEY come to me in yearning dreams,
　　Afar I see them stand :
One day I, too, shall see them,
　　Living in their own land.

The bright eyes of the poets
　　Shine from that glorious sphere ;
And artists, dream enraptured, say
　　The Beautiful is here.

There art thou, Virgin-Mother,
　　And thou next glorified,
O young inspired heroine,
　　That mid the red flames died !

And martyr-maidens pallid-browed,
  Christ's lilies stedfast-hearted,
With the very smile upon their lips
  They wore as they departed.

They who commune with each other
  Downward from age to age,
With the same great book before them
  Unfolding page by page.

Interpreters of that great song
  God has written in the skies,
Beholding in the peopled dust
  Divinest mysteries :—

The Beautiful, the Glorious :—
  How fast the vision fills !
O fold of God, take me too in,
  Lost out upon the hills !

AN ORPHAN.

Lying on thy little bed,
Still and pale, as thou wert dead ;
On thy arm thy drooping head
    Has sunk down wearily :
In a deep exhausted sleeping,
After tempest-floods of weeping,
Fall'n into the angels' keeping ;
    For no friend else is nigh.
Ever in the narrow room
Colder and colder falls the gloom ;
The evening darkens, and the rain
Beats on the narrow lattice-pane ;
And the one grey poplar, shaking
By the window, ever making
Mournful music to thy waking,
    Rocks its shadow by.
All things round are bare and rough,
But thou art soft and young enough

For tenderer comforting and cheer
Than any that thou findest here,
    Under the cold, strange sky.

Life has come on thee unawares,
In a cold flood of griefs and cares ;
Troubled thou art and desolate
In mind and body, and estate,
    And spent with misery.
In thy helpless softness thrown
Out upon the world alone ;
Only faces all unknown,
    To meet thee carelessly ;
Stranger speech within thy ears,
Bread of exile and of tears ;
And no memory of sweet years
    To console thy pain ;
And in thy heart-broken sorrow,
No good visions of to-morrow
    Thy patience to sustain.
Prayers are darkly drowned in doubt,
And the heavens are blotted out
    By the blinding rain :
In thy anguish left so lonely,
Is but one hope for thee only,
    Never to wake again.

Thou sleepest softly now, and yet
Thy eyelashes are freshly wet,
And on thy cheeks two tears are set,
As if thy dreams could not forget :—
    But who will care for these ?
As they are so they must be,
No one will kiss them away for thee,
    Lying there until they freeze.
All around thee golden-rare,
The heavy loosen'd rain of hair,
With a mantle royal-fair,
    Enfoldeth thee to rest.
Soft young hands and fair of mould,
Small as a child's ten years old,
As white as snowflakes and as cold,
    Are folded on thy breast ;
Together passionately entwin'd,
As they had sought about to find
Some caress of tender kind,
And meeting none of sister or mother,
Are tightly clasp'd in one another
    With yearning mournfullest :
Fingers not chisell'd out of stone,
But like white roses at sunrise blown,
Into that shape and sculpture grown,
    By angel fingers prest.

Thy brows are calm at last in sleep,
But, haunted still with pain, they keep
A shadowy look, so dark and deep,
Whoso beholdeth can but weep,
    But thou still slumberest.

The silent sadness of thy face
Thrills like a sighing through the place ;
Yet thanks at least be for the grace
Of this hour's quiet breathing-space
    Amid the waters wild.
Though thy young heart in its breaking
Sees it not, yet unforsaking
Christ o'er thee a hush is making
    To give thee slumber mild :
He giveth His beloved sleep :
    He loveth thee, poor child !

ADELAIDE.

PART I.

A YEAR, it is not a year ago
Since he came, who loved me so,
Where I lay in the primroses low
    Moaning my complaint :
For the fate fixed for me ere I was born,
Away in the cloister, lonely and lorn,
I that was full of the fire and the morn,
    And for yearning of Life grew faint.

I with my long hair's golden grace,
And the flickering Northern Lights in my face,
Over the snow, and my pride of race,
    Of Suabian ancestry,
Queenlike stature, and moulded limb ;
Yet not worthy withal of him ;—
The dark-eyed artist whom God sent forth
Over the mountains into the North,
    That he there might light on me.

Adelaide.

He met me there in the April wood,
It was not long ere we understood
   How our hearts had fated been.
O sweet young spring days, so fresh and cool,
Each hour more green and more beautiful,
When the flowers were waking up from sleep,
And the birds sang all together to keep
   Our whispers safe within.

What were all those words he said?
What were those sweet words murmurèd
   Under the boughs enlaced?
I cannot tell—some sounds remain,
Some echoes, only not so plain,
   Come sighing o'er the waste.
'Alas! O motherless fair child,
Yearning against the world so wild,'
   A voice was wont to say —
'I know the darkness of thy fate
Is bound upon thee as a weight,
   That grows more crushing day by day.
There is no pride, there is no scorn
   In all thy stateliness, my queen,
The light beneath those eyelids born,
When Love himself at last shall dawn,
   Shall meet him trustful and serene.'

And more and more—that voice flowed on
Like silver streams beneath the sun.
Ah ! already my heart was won,
Perhaps too lightly, perhaps too soon,
   But it was his for ever.
And if we each did love so well,
Could any sorrow that befell
   Our hearts hereafter sever ?

And so it came, that one night late,
I went forth from my father's gate,
   All trembling and alone ;
With all my dowry, my gold hair,—
And stole past moonlit pathways fair,
In shadow, breathless and aware,
Through tangled woods, where May's first air
   Breathed in the midnight tone.
And on that midnight still and lone,
In a grey chapel, overgrown
   With ivy, by the stream,
With ruined arches overhead,
And glimmering lights, the words were said
That made us one, and we were wed.—
   Ah, still it haunts my dream !—
As down the river, amid the balm
Of the May birthnight our boat went calm,

And I lay half in swoon.
The full moon with the face of a saint,
Looked on us as in benison;
Sweet voices from the convent choir
Chanted the midnight orison;
It floated over the waters dim,
As we went gliding on.

We travelled in fear, we travelled fast,
Till danger of pursuit was past;
Then freedom and love had come at last.
They say that it was deadly sin,
But nothing told me so within.
Onward we went, hand in hand,
Through the warm and sunny land;
Never was seen, by sea or shore,
A spring so beautiful before:
The hawthorn boughs dropt show'rings sweet,
Of snowy petals at our feet;
It was a still suspended rain
Of beauty betwixt earth and tree;
The blossom-clusters hung in vain,
A veil across the mystery
Of the green wood-worlds we past thro',
And sunny orchards, where the dew
Still on the lush grass lay.

Purple veins of violets
Ran like dark-blue rivulets
   Winding thro' the moss away ;
Wild white stars from the dark woods gleam'd ;
   Blue eyes from the hedgebanks laugh'd at me ;
And the sunward opening valleys seem'd
   All robed in a blossom-lace to be.

Wondrous liquid strains of song
Through the leaves trill'd loud and long
   From the nightingale's wild heart ;
Madly darting high and low,
Running all the compass through,
   In silver notes apart :
With sudden passion bursting free,
Into a flood of melody,
Rising, soaring, shrill and clear,
Falling soft as the fall of a tear,
While we held our breath to hear
   Under the leaves.

And little children gazed at me
With eyes that were full of wonder and glee ;
   Then ran to their cottage-door and cried,
'O mother ! mother ! come and see !

Adelaide.

The princess with the golden hair,
   Is come from the enchanted hall,
And the knight who broke the spell is there,
   They are passing this way side by side ;
     It is all true ! How beautiful !'

Deeper into the summer
   We wander'd every day ;
There lay a thicker shadow
   Over the grassy way.
Untir'd wayfarers, when the Moon
Of Flowers was passing into June,
From dawn till evening came too soon ;
Till in the east the stars were rising,
   And the west lay still a golden sea,
And suddenly thrill'd by the chiming
   Of the Vesper-Bell's far melody.
Oh, prayer and praise were easy then !
   Our prayers were all of charity
For the wide world of fellow-men,
   That were not richly blest as we.
And the world lay around us there,
With its great mountains in the air,
Slowly drawn near for us to climb,
In all its beauty and its prime :—
O love, that was our Eden time !

Across the mountains journey'd we,
And entered into Italy;
And through enchanted pathways past
To Florence, and were home at last.
I had had dreams of heaven before,
But now my heart was running o'er,
And satisfied for evermore,
   So rapt in love were we.

Part II.

When the November darkness fell,
That year on Florence came as well
A deadly fever,—and he died :
I could not save him at his side ;
So suddenly he sank away,
Nor had the strength farewell to say,
And from the heavens died out the day.

I watched beside him a night and a day,
   With strangely beating and burning brow,
I sat and gazed on the lifeless clay,
   It was all that earth held for me now.
It was a wild and stormy night
   For a soul to go forth all alone ;

There was no moon or stars to light
  The staircase up to the great throne;
But the fierce winds were blowing all abroad,
And the blinding rain in torrents pour'd
    Through the blackness of the sky;
And moaning voices went thro' the air,
With sounds as of spirits wailing there,
  And sometimes a piercing shriek swept by,
    And howls of demons' strife;
  All the lights of heaven and the saints on high
    Were blotted out of life;
  I, only I, a living curse,
  In all the dead dark universe.
The wet panes glimmer'd all shining and black,
  And fearful faces were looking in,
But never his face to mine looked back,
  Through all the horror and whirl and din.
When broke the chilly morning light
My hair hung round me, grisly-white.

And so the day came round again;
A day of dearirness and rain ;—
The withered leaves against the pane
Rattled in their death-agony
Ere the blast whirled them from the tree.

The dead within, and the storm without;
  One all raving, and one at rest :—
Never a ray of sun in the south,
  Never a ray of hope in my breast.

  When a night and a day had come and gone,
  And the face of the dead was beginning to change,
  Suddenly I heard below
  Sounds of strange voices,—no, not strange!
  If my heart could have sunk more low,
  It had sunk then, to find them near,
  My kindred who had track'd me here,
  As bloodhounds track a wounded deer.
  And I, who had been motherless,
  Whose childhood had known no caress,
  Nor comforting in sicknesses,
    Gazed on them in despair.
  Of their reproaches and their scorn
  I little heeded—I had borne
  Too much,—yet one so all-forlorn
    They might have known to spare.
  They took me—I, who had no friend
  To help, whose life was at an end,
  Back to my cloister'd doom to spend
    The long death-anguish there.

So back by the same roads we past
We travelled in the summer last.
We came by winter and by night;
The mountains were so ghastly white,
  Like shrouded giants stiff and cold,
    The grimness of their stony sleep
  In freezing distance to behold
    Made all my veins with horror creep.

And now I am here, and I do not know
Whether I am mad or no;
They have cut off all my long bright hair,
They have taken the ring he gave me to wear,
And a fever runs thro' me, nerve and brain,
Consuming me ever with fire and pain;
I sicken and sicken day by day,
Pining to death in prison away;
Through the hateful round of the daily rule,
With nought that is free or beautiful,
Through the lonely nights in my narrow cell,
Through the hopeless years stretching forwards still,
One voice rings ever and everywhere,
O lost for ever! despair! despair!

Oh let me die, and feel no more!
What does this sickness come before?

M

Could I too die and pass?
This burning pain is all too strong;
How long, O cruel heavens! how long
　　Will you so close, alas?
What matters it unto despair,
Whether death cometh foul or fair
　　To lead us to the tomb?
Only come soon, that I may know
The best or worst of joy or woe
　　That waits me as my doom!
A year ago I was a child,
I remember the young face that smiled
　　From the mirror back to me:
Now I can feel the hollows deep,
And dark lines worn by lack of sleep
Under the eyes that fain would weep
　　To loose their misery.

My strength is failing from me fast,
I think that I shall die at last.
So lonely!—oh! I stood by thee
Belovèd, in thine agony!
I did not shrink for fear or woe,
Thy heart and mine the secret know.

And wilt thou not then near me be
When the solemn hour comes to me ?
It will not be terrible to thee,
For thou art where they feel no pain,
And thy heart can never ache again.
   I know I would descend from heaven,
      To dwell in hell, if thou wert there ;
     Look down then from thy bright place given,
      And comfort me in my despair !
Hold me one moment to thy breast,
And say farewell—then I could rest.

O my belovèd, my noble one !
Such a little time we had in the sun !
O glorious eyes, so tender and true,
Look but once the dark midnight through !
O voice of mine, so tender and sweet,
That ever my coming step would greet,
And sent through my heart such keen delight ;—
It flashes back through the lonely night !
Alas ! where am I ?   It is gone ;
O stay with me,—I am alone !
Nay, think not thus to cheat thy pain,
He will never, never, come back again !

Part III.

The frost is broken off the plain,
The young year is come round again,
   And the sun shines afar.
Like shadows over the long grass,
Sweet thoughts come over me and pass,
   Ere I know what or whence they are.
My brain is weak, I scarce can see,
But strange sweet voices speak to me;
   And without visible sign or token
Save the sweet voices of the earth
In summer's melody and mirth,
   God's spirit to my soul hath spoken,
      And to my spirit brought the calm,
   And to my heart, that erst was broken,
      The precious slumber-balm.

Ah me, my race is nearly run!
How little have I served or done
Here in the world beneath the sun:
   God's mercy be my stay!

I was but given little grace
Whereby we take heroic place;
Nothing of that strength of heart
Which makes a triumph of each part;
    And at the close of day,
As after weary ways a child
Comes to its father reconciled
    By love and trust alone,
So I go forth my Lord to meet,
Laying my heart before His feet,
    Its suffering all its crown.

Love, we two shall meet otherwhere!
    O love, it will not be so long!
    Love is immortal, love is strong,
Stronger than death, and than despair:
For despair hath been, and is now forgot,
And death is here, but I heed him not,
For I am coming, coming to thee!
I wait till the veil falls off, to see
    Thine eyes of eager welcoming—
And love is shining so clear and bright,
That my soul needeth no other light;
    Then love, thou hast the triumphing!

The air is balmy-warm in May,
The days are lengthening to the day
    When all the shadows cease.
They are more kind and gentle now;
For the great Angel on my brow
    Has set the mark of peace.
He cometh on with sleep and rest;
Take me, belovèd, to thy breast;
    The stilly night is falling;
With closèd eyes and silent soul,
I hear as some great organ's roll
    Over the waters calling.
The sweet heavens open evermore,
Christ stands beside the open door
    To let me enter in;
I can but fold my hands, and part
With a deep trust within my heart
    That love at last shall win.